Monique Schwitter was born in 1972 in Zurich and now lives and works in Hamburg. Between 1993 and 1997 she studied acting and directing at the Mozarteum University of Dramatic Arts in Salzburg and went on to perform in Zurich, Frankfurt and Graz. In 2005 she published her first volume of short stories, *Wenn's schneit beim Krokodil* (When *It Snows at the Crocodile's*), for which she was awarded the 2006 Robert Walser Prize for the best literary debut of the year and the Förderpreis der Schweizer Schillerstiftung (2006). Her novel *Ohren haben keine Lider* (*Ears have no Lids*) was published in 2008, and her collection of short stories *Goldfischgedächtnis* was awarded the Rotahornpreis in 2011.

Eluned Gramich was born in west Wales and has lived in England, Japan and Germany. She now works as a writer and translator.

Goldfish Memory

Goldfish Memory

A Collection of Short Stories
by Monique Schwitter

Translated from the German
by Eluned Gramich

Parthian, Cardigan SA43 1ED
www.parthianbooks.com
First published in 2015
© Monique Schwitter 2015
© Translation by Eluned Gramich 2015
ISBN 978-1-910409-63-3
Cover design by Claire Houguez
Typeset by Elaine Sharples
Printed and bound by Edwards Brothers Malloy
Published with the financial support of the Welsh Books Council
British Library Cataloguing in Publication Data
A cataloguing record for this book is available from the British Library.

Contents

Memories beautify life, but only forgetting makes it bearable.
Honore de Balzac

All the things one has forgotten cry for help in one's dreams.
Elias Canetti.

Our Story

It's the mother who opens the door for me. *It's you.* Just two words, delivered in the professional tone of an accomplished secretary. *Please come in.* A quick but refined smile distorts her face, as if she'd hurriedly put on an ill-fitting pig's snout, before it disappears. There one second, gone the next. Out of nowhere. She shows me in, even though I know the way. *Charlotte's been waiting.* The accusation is impossible to ignore. *I'm on time,* I reply, reacting to her secretarial tone, which makes her turn to look at me pityingly. I can smell Chanel No.19 and cigarette smoke, both of which seem to be streaming from her pearl-decorated ears.

Charlotte's bald head has shrunk again. I'm visibly taken aback, but smile quickly, wishing that it could hide my shock, wishing that it could erase the whole situation, the shrunken head, the reason for my visit and, if possible, her mother too.

It seems to work – partly anyway – her mother *finally leaves us alone.* The threatening undertone, the Chanel No.19 and the smell of cigarette smoke linger behind in the room for a few minutes.

You look great! Charlotte beams at me. Her skin hasn't shrunk – or maybe it's doing so more slowly than her head – it's wrapped itself in deep creases around her mouth and eyes, which stand out bluer than usual against the sallow wrinkles. *Rubbish,* I say as grumpily as I always do when she talks nonsense in her little girl's voice. *Stop it, my beauty years are definitely over now. I look like shit and feel wonderful.*

I love you. She shakes her head, moved.

You get on my nerves with your silly talk, I grumble, hug her and kiss her fleetingly, as always. *How much time do we have?* My question sounds like something her mother would say. *Ben's getting picked up at four.* And straightaway she adds: *Do you want to see an up-to-date photo?*

No, I answer darkly. *Thanks a lot, dear Lottie. You know kids' photos put me in a bad mood.*

Alright. She's deeply offended. *Let's start. Did you bring everything with you?*

I nod, take my bag from my shoulder and get the notepad out. *Just a moment,* she says, *I'll be right back.* She leaves the room and closes the door. The sound of her footsteps quickly recedes. After a while, she turns on a tap and starts coughing – in the bathroom, I guess. And how she coughs! She doesn't stop. She constantly produces the same sound, and it's the monotony and duration of it which makes it so distressing. For something to do, I desperately try to think of what this monotonous coughing reminds me of: the final dying noises of an old ship's engine. Once, on the Mekong river, I listened to a similar sound for what seemed like hours, before everything fell silent and I realised, like all the other passengers, that our boat trip had come to an end. Lottie stops coughing. I can't hear anything anymore. My heart races; it's like someone is trying to strangle me from behind. I've got to pull myself together to stop myself from getting up to look for her.

She silently opens the door. She pushes her bald skull inside and grins at me with her wrinkled mouth. *It's me again.*

"This is the story of Marie and Charlotte," she says, dictating. *Of Charlotte and Marie,* I interrupt.

You always want to decide everything!

I thought I was the writer.

She looks at me so sadly that I have to laugh. *Fine, carry on with the dictation,* I sigh and grip the pen.

"It began ten years ago on the 20th of August. Of course, it was me who spoke to her first."

Could you please tell it from a third person's perspective? I ask her, and I write down: "Of course it was Charlotte who first spoke to Marie." Lottie looks at me defiantly. *Alright,* she says and continues angrily, "Nice to meet you, says Charlotte. Nice to meet you, answers Marie."

Ever since primary school, it has never ceased to surprise me how much one can do, dream, accomplish during a dictation. I realise now, for instance, that in my mind's eye I'm going through the photographs of our shared history, which are still in my bag, and as I go through them one after another I observe Charlotte and compare her to the Charlotte who spoke to me on the street, almost ten years ago.

Hello!

Hello.

I'm on my way to the park.

Nice.

Today is a day for eating ice cream in the park.

Have fun.

A day for eating ice cream and talking. Fancy it?

I don't think so.

I think so. I had to laugh at that. Her blue eyes beamed at me. *Nice to meet you,* she said. *Nice to meet you,* I replied, defeated.

I'd never eaten such good ice cream before. But I'd often

sat on park benches. I'd never sat with a strange woman, whom I'd simply followed, before. I'd been with men whom I didn't trust, because they showed their interest in me so openly. I'd once sworn always to avoid women with little girl's voices. I'd never liked a person I'd just met so much before.

Her appearance – as I squint at her through half-open eyes, my right hand following her dictation – causes a familiar itch on the tip of my nose, which will, as a general rule, be followed by tears. She looks so lost without hair, with this tiny head and the shrunken, wrinkled face; at one moment an old woman, at the next almost a baby, without age or gender; at first glance, she's only recognisably female through prior knowledge or at close quarters.

You haven't interrupted me for a long time, she complains and looks at me challengingly. I almost write this sentence down too. *I don't have any objections,* I reply. *Please carry on. You talk, I'll write.*

"The two of them had only known each other for a short time, before Charlotte got into urgent difficulties and had to ask her newly-made friend for help in the middle of the night."

My goodness, how unbearably Charlotte can get on my nerves! Actually, it did start like that, when I hardly knew her name. She called me at three in the morning in a panic. *I have no idea what to do, I think I'm pregnant! But its not Klaus's! It's Orkan's – probably!*

Who's Orkan? Wait, I've got to put the light on, I can't find my glasses. It's weird, but I can't listen without my glasses on, least of all think.

Have you done a test?

No.

So why do you think you're pregnant then?

4

I dreamt about it.

Sorry?

Actually, I dreamt that Orkan did it on purpose.

I haven't got a clue who Orkan is, nor do I want to know who he is tonight. Please never phone me at three in the morning again. If you do, you'll regret it. Good night.

I heard nothing from her for a week. She was offended. Then she wrote me a inordinately long, angry letter, which was, for the most part, unreadable. Finally, she invited me to eat ice cream and forgave me. Until the next night-time phone call.

My Slutty-Lottie seems asexual now, but her behaviour over the last ten years, her amorous intrigues and entanglements, was intensely sexual.

I wouldn't want to burden you with it if I had the choice, but Klaus is killing me!

I thought you broke up with him.

Exactly.

What happened?

I survived, thank God.

Lottie, for God's sake, what is it?

I'm scared!

Then come over.

I can't, Bernd is here.

Who's Bernd?

I've told you about it, it's a recent thing, she whispered. *And he's really nice! I can't talk right now you know, but he's really—*

Great, then Bernd can protect you in case Klaus turns up with an axe. Why did you call me?

Just listen for a second!

No, I'm hanging up now and going back to sleep!

How often I was annoyed with her! How often she scared me by telling me that her life hung in the balance, that she had cancer, that she wanted to kill herself. I feel wild rage shooting through my belly when I think about it; a rage as new, as young, as stubborn as a child's, learning to walk. Even now I could grab her shrunken head and bang it against the wall, if it had hair I could hold on to. *The grip is missing,* I mumble, and Lottie stares at me, surprised. *Nothing, nothing,* I say. In any case, she's familiar with it: my indistinct, lost-in-thought mumbling, and she smiles indulgently before continuing, and what she says is:

"We occasionally struck a wrong note, but there was never discord. Rather, between the two women there was a deep mysterious bond from the beginning, a kind of silent understanding that they would stand by each other in every circumstance, free each other from every tricky situation, alleviate every hardship."

Her words strike hard. Considering the present circumstances, it sounds like a taunt. I look up quickly. But Charlotte, with her eyes closed and her dreamy smile, is stuck deep in our past. "Each of us knew that the other was always there, at any time of day, for any problem, anything at all."

How many times she begged me to lie for her when I was asked where she was at a particular time. Or for me to phone her employer and play the gravely-sick sister, whose last wish is to die with her close family around her, making it imperative that Charlotte come immediately and stand by me in those dark hours. If I were brave enough, which I'd like to be, I'd interrupt her now and remind her of this story in detail: this story of the dying sister, the one which allowed her to go for a week's holiday in the Maldives with a lover, and which I made possible with my false phone call to her boss, and where, for two months after, she grieved in the office, teary-eyed and dressed in black. If I were brave, I'd ask her whether she still believes now that it was acceptable to think up such a story. If, in her eyes, it was worth the holiday to the Maldives. But I think I know the answer. *Yes*, she'd say, and again, for the last time, she'd describe the grain of the Maldive sand, how it works as a beautifier on the body, running and rolling across it, and how she'd never felt, nor would ever feel, her skin so soft.

Can we take a short break? I've got to take my medication.

Of course! I put down the pen and stretch my writing hand.

The previous scene repeats itself. Charlotte opens the door, closes the door; I hear nothing, only, this time, her mother silently enters the room. I look up as the No.19 drifts towards me. She's holding a tray in her hands, with two cups and a glass bowl, and she gives me a searching look.

Is it going well? She wants to know. *Yes, thank you.* I search my notes for a foothold. *I think we should have a chat.* This is how security guards talk to female shoplifters. I start up at once. *What about?* I ask, panicked, because just the idea of having to talk to her alone is torture. She draws nearer. The cups on the tray clatter. Her look darkens with every step. She stands up close in front of me and I can smell the cold smoke from her mouth (it definitely comes from her mouth and not from her ears). *My daughter is dying,* she hisses in a painstakingly composed voice, with a piercing look. *Yes,* I mumble quietly and nod, my eyes averted. Charlotte stands in the doorway. She is just as pale as her mother and looks at me in a similarly searching way. *Thanks, Mum, looks delicious,* she says then, untroubled as a freshly hatched butterfly, and takes the tray from her mother.

It's a special herbal mix, she explains, as she takes the

teacups from the tray. *A magic potion, which will let me get as old as my Granny, who's celebrating her hundredth birthday in September. It's in the family, everyone gets really old.* I sip it. *It tastes like bile!*

Yes, but it helps.

She places her hand on my arm and presses it as if she were playing the piano. She's been doing it to get my attention since I've known her; she taps my arm with her cold, hard fingers, lightly at first, and then increasingly harder, until she finally grips my arm so tightly that I protest and have to free it from its prison.

Your magic potion, she cries. *Do you still remember?*

I do, Lottie, I reply. The affair is still embarrassing to me. *Do you think it belongs in our story?*

Absolutely!

I pick up the pen: *Then fire away. But from the beginning.*

"It was a stormy night in March a few years back, when Charlotte phoned her friend and told her, 'We have to talk'.

'I'm working.'

'Oh, a male visitor.'

'You're confusing me with yourself. I'm just working.'

'It's urgent,' Charlotte remained persistent, 'could you please come over for a bit?'

'No. You want to talk, so you can come to me.'

'It's stormy. It's raining. It's horrible outside and my car won't start!'

'You're really shameless.'

'I've just cooked something delicious!' It was spinach pie. Marie was in a bad mood. 'This is the last time,' she warned, 'in the future, I'll be charging you for my time. Twenty euros an hour.' Charlotte refilled their plates and said, 'Just stop talking and eat. It's only twelve euros.' She laughed for so long that at some point Marie joined in, a little annoyed at first, but gradually she laughed almost as freely. In the middle of our fun, Charlotte said suddenly, 'I don't want to be depressed at forty and kill myself at forty-two. So. I need a man, because I need a child.' Her friend didn't understand. 'You have so many men, you could fill a whole classroom with them!' But Charlotte was determined not only to become a mother, but a wife, too, and among the many ranks of lovers, there was, in her opinion, no suitable candidate despite having tried so hard to recall the years of ecstatic, physical wrestling, to remember every lover, if not their complete appearance and full names, at least a few details. 'One was called George, and there was that one with the unbelievably long toes, and one, an Austrian, who had freckles everywhere.'

"But all the body parts she brought to mind didn't help; he, the future husband and father, was not among them. 'It's better this way than if I thought of someone whose phone number I couldn't find anymore,' decided Charlotte. The relationship should be 'nice and simple', 'clear, neat, official.' So, now comes the snag, obviously only a long-distance relationship could be considered. 'Long-distance?' 'Exactly.' With a man who was too involved in his career to get onto a plane every weekend and visit his wife and child. It was more than enough to meet up once or twice a month. Where should she find such a man? How could she find the time, where could she get the money to travel that far and meet him? Marie asked for 'dessert. Coffee. Schnapps. I've got to think.' 'I love you,' said Charlotte. Whereupon Marie answered, harshly, 'Oh just leave me alone. Bring me pen and paper.'"

Yes, that's what it had been like; she'd recounted it pretty accurately. After three glasses of Schnapps, I circled eight words on a piece of paper, pushed it towards her and said, *Today is Tuesday. I think we'll be in time for the weekend edition of this broadsheet newspaper from Bavaria you can buy everywhere. Here is the notice:*

Beautiful, cultured woman in her thirties
seeks rich academic for children.

Lottie was sceptical at first, but she sent the newspaper ad the very next morning and received a letter within a few days in which the national broadsheet newspaper communicated the fact that unfortunately they were unable to publish it. The personal section served to initiate a two-person relationship. Our notice, however, did not clearly state that a relationship, *per se*, was desired. Only an interest in a financially powerful father was made clear.

Charlotte changed 'children' to 'marriage' and submitted the notice again. She received forty-seven letters, which we examined over several evenings. Some had attached photos – we immediately discounted them – and Lottie phoned some while I was there, asking questions I wrote down and pushed towards her. In my opinion, there was no one suitable, but she arranged to meet five candidates. She chose Daniel after she'd met up and slept with two others. Unfortunately, she never went into much detail about these meetings, and she doesn't go into it now either. Back then she only told me, shaking her head, she'd drawn a couple of blanks. Today she dictates, skipping over the blanks: "And so Charlotte met Daniel and thought, this could be something." It became something, although, since their meetings rarely coincided with her more fertile days, she didn't get pregnant for months. And now that awful magic potion comes into play, which – I can only shake my head even though it was years ago now – I brewed for Lottie. Me! Me, who is sceptical about the effect of every herb – except for a few dried plants and leaves, which are apparently ecstatically effective. Not that I care. Apart from that, I don't believe that they could prevent any misfortune or bring about any kind of good luck on earth, whether they're cut up small, or plucked bare, or dried or quick-frozen. That's my opinion. So I appointed myself the task of amassing the selected herbs, pouring hot water at ninety degrees over them, soaking them for seventeen minutes, draining, boiling again and, after adding more ingredients, letting it boil for hours until it formed a thick liquid. At the end I even – cluelessly, I admit, but very determinedly – cast a spell. Lottie drank it and fell pregnant the next day. Even though it was, in purely mathematical terms, impossible. Since then she claims I have *the gift*. The more she praises me for that past witchcraft, the more deeply I feel I've failed, because to this day I haven't been able to brew a potion to cure the rank growth of her tissue. As if she can read my thoughts, she stops dictating, sips the herbal tea which will make her reach a hundred, and looks at me, earnest and stern, over the rim of her cup. I take off my glasses and return the look.

A knock. *Coming, Mummy, we'll have a short break soon,* calls Lottie towards the door – the handle has already been pressed down – actually managing to stave off a renewed appearance of her mother, who is, in my eyes, anything but a 'Mummy'. The door handle goes up again and nothing else happens. *We'd better eat some of this cake,* Lottie takes the glass bowl with the thin, dark brown things from the tray. *Better for whom?* I want to know. She shrugs and takes a bite.

Disgusting, she says, and with the word hundreds of fine crumbs fall out of her mouth.

My God, the photos, she looks at me like she's just remembered that Ben has been waiting for hours to be picked up. *You've got them with you, right?* As soon as I hand them to her, it's as if all her worries are wiped away; the wrinkled mouth pulls into a happy grin. *No!* She says. *Just look at that! Can you believe it?* I took the photo the night before Ben was born. Lottie stretches her gigantic belly primly towards the camera as if she's trying to enter through the lens, belly-first, backed up by the kind of look a provoked lioness would make just before attacking the observer: 'I'll eat you up', the look and the belly seem to say, and even now I feel it's directed towards me. Lottie laughs wildly and doesn't want to let go of the belly-photo. *Here, you cow,* I hand her the next photo, *Carnival, you put your tongue in my mouth and danced Samba in it!* She beams. *I just wanted to know what it would feel like,* she says. And she leafs through the pile, deep in happiness, shaking her head now and again with an expression I've never seen before, somewhere between being overwhelmed, disbelief, joy and sorrow: she bursts out laughing, falls silent, smiles sweetly, strokes a picture with her finger, suddenly closes her eyes. *You'll never forget me, hm?* She asks, and knows the answer, because she says it with me as I answer: *No.* Like a shadow, her 'no' follows on the heels of mine. She opens her eyes and says: *I know you don't like to hear it, but I love you, really.*

I lose control and tear open the door. I run across the landing, past her mother, who stands motionlessly in my way, to the bathroom, where I turn on the tap. Protected by the flow of water, I let my tears fall. Even after a few minutes I can still feel her mother's piercing gaze on my back. I wipe away the tears, turn around angrily and return just as piercing a stare.

My mother wants to kill me, says Lottie as I re-enter the room, one of the dark brown biscuits in her hand. *I'm choking!*

Then I'll sacrifice myself and eat them all, give it here, I reply and grab the glass bowl. *No way!* She shouts, *I won't allow it! Hands off!* She holds the bowl with both hands.

No, I want it! I pull the bowl.

No it's mine! She holds it tightly.

Damn it, let me die, I hastily stick two pieces in my mouth at once.

Me, me, I want to die, Lottie protests and three pieces disappear into her mouth. And at some point the bowl is empty. *Very good,* Lottie is satisfied. *Now my mother's world is alright again. As long as her baking gets eaten, all is well.*

Suddenly disappointed, she points at the photo and says in her little girl's voice, *but there aren't any of the wedding.*

Lottie, I wasn't at your wedding. She looks at me disbelievingly. *I was sick.*

I'd forgotten that. She is just as disappointed now as back then, when I phoned up and cancelled because I was in bed with an ear infection. She sighs deeply. *What a shame. And were you really sick?*

Yes.

Honestly?

Lottie, if I ever lied in the past then, really, it was always for you. Charlotte is ill. Charlotte's sister is dying. Charlotte's child has just been run over I'm afraid she can't come, please understand...

Sh! Lottie points to the door.

Behind it is silence. *Back to the story,* she demands, looking at her watch: *God, we've got to hurry. I think we've got to shorten it otherwise we won't get it all down by four.* She sits

13

down properly. *Where were we? The magic potion. I became pregnant, right. And you sent me this unbelievable bouquet of roses.*

Please, we can skip that, you wanted to shorten it.

I won't sacrifice the roses.

Why are you so obsessed with the roses?

I rarely give her presents, it's true. She always showed me small kindnesses. I'd go to the toilet and on my return I'd find a chocolate heart or a note with the words 'I love you' on it, or a cutesy keyring with a talking bear, 'Forget me not'. I hated these offerings and told her so: *Stop doing this,* I asked her a dozen times.

Can't, you're my friend.

I'll only stay your friend if you stop with this rubbish!

It didn't help. We both remained stubborn. I worry that she never understood what and who she is to me, because I never dressed up my feelings with gifts.

Now would be the moment to tell her. I like you, Lottie. Oh, what the hell, I more than like you. No, I think a lot of you – to hell with all these clichéd phrases. There are cleverer, more interesting, more sensible, more just women than you Lottie who, at some point, have offered their friendship – no, that doesn't work either. So I say: *carry on dictating, Lottie, with the roses if need be.*

And she goes on, telling our story, which I write down word for word, during which my own thoughts and memories come to me. Her pregnancy was dramatic. It ended up in a fall down the stairs and bleeding, the cause of which I didn't understand, but I drove her to the hospital and waited for hours in admissions before she was given the all clear. I was quite astonished that Ben came into the world healthy and, from the moment I met him, I'm afraid I couldn't stand him.

He looks more and more like his father every day, by the way. Whom I also dislike. Luckily I rarely see him because most of what Lottie wished for came true. Most of it. She has a child, she has a man, who is relatively solvent, a workaholic academic. She has her long-distance relationship. But she hadn't counted on her mother moving in. Her mother is the housekeeper, nursery maid, manager: the guardian and a hound from hell.

The dictation has reached Ben's fourth birthday a few months ago. Lottie had already been ill for a year. The story of her illness has no place in the story of Charlotte and Marie. All the same, I have to weave into the account of Ben's birthday that despite the fact that Lottie was thin, wizened and bald, she was still full of hope for recovery. We drove Ben and some other children to the water-park. Lottie gave the children over to the pre-booked Party Organiser and gestured for me to follow her. She'd put on a bathing-turban and wore a colourful, sequined swimming costume with 'Push-Up Zones' which should have given her some curves. She looked like a lost Amazonian parrot and she excitedly flapped her arms in a similar way. *Yes, over there!* She pointed at some of the deck-chairs, *they're waiting for us!* She took a bottle of fizz out of her huge beach bag and two plastic cups. *Since my mother moved in, I've had so few opportunities,* she says after the first gulp. On cue, the lifeguard appeared. *I'm sorry but you can't eat or drink here. Please enjoy your beverage in our Food Service Area.*

But then I can't talk to you!

The lifeguard was confused. So was I, but Lottie pressed on: *Sit next to me for a second.* She handed me the bottle and I went to the restaurant, where I drained cup after cup alone as I watched Lottie and the lifeguard through the window.

15

They had a lot to say to each other. And there was a lot to laugh about. Suddenly they vanished. After half an hour, Lottie appeared just as suddenly at my table and said: *You're pretty drunk.*

And you're pretty brazen. Was it worth it?

She magicked another bottle of fizz from her bag and downed three cupfuls. *Have a go, come on!* And we both swayed our way, one after the other, up the ladder of the Big Tunnel Slide and sped down, hand in hand, and with each go we screamed louder and held on tighter. She lost her turban and countless sequins. I sustained just as many bruises, but we'd never have stopped had Ben not stood in front of us and said, *Mama, the woman says the party's over.*

I think that's it, says Lottie with another look at her watch. *What do you think? It's finished. That's our story. Did you write everything down? The story ends here. Before we start crying.* She places her hand on my arm, perhaps for the last time, and, hitting the keys hard, plays piano until her fingers grip my flesh and come to rest. *Agreed?* She asks.

I look through the pages of our story while thinking if there's anything else to say.

A month ago, the doctors found the metastasis in her lung. Since then it's all happened very quickly. *Before we start cry*ing, reminds Lottie, and I put the notepad away and smile at her. It's her mother who saves me. She knocks curtly, opening the door at the same time and says, *it's time to go.* She means, it's time for me to go. She says it in a way which doesn't allow for either delay or contradiction, so I put my jacket on obediently and shoulder my bag. And then she says it. Lottie: *Farewell.* And her mother leads me to the door.

Haiku and Horror

She thinks it might get tricky.

She mixes another instant coffee. She sprays the telephone receiver with disinfectant. She cleans the gaps between her teeth. She dials the number, hears it ring and hangs up.

She notes down the time on the notepad in front of her, and crosses it out again after sliding the tip of her tongue over every single tooth, as if checking that they are all there and in their place.

*

Redial.

Ringing.

Heavy breathing. His voice is hoarse.

– Did I wake you?

– You have my number?

– I'm a journalist.

– Perhaps you know how I can overcome the horror of seeing my own face in the morning?

– No.

– Thanks for your help.

He hangs up.
She throws the pen on the floor and swears.

*

A woman's voice. – Yes?
– Good morning. I'd like to speak with Mr Brandtner.
– He's gone out.
– He was there a moment ago.
   (With a strained voice) – He's gone out.
   (Terribly polite) – Could you just hand me over please?
   The woman (who is she? The housekeeper? Niece? Carer?
Secretary?) holds her hand over the receiver. For a few
moments, there is hardly any sound, then the line crackles.
He must have violently wrenched the phone from his
'colleague'.
– Listen, you're wasting your time!
– Not at all.
– You're getting on my nerves!
– I'm sorry.
– I'm hanging up. Please leave me alone. I'm tired; I'm in a
   bad mood; I've got bad breath.

*

It rings. Five times. The answer machine springs on, an
automatic voice speaks. Unfortunately no one is at home.
– Good morning Mr Brandtner. I'm looking forward to your
   call. Please find my number at the head of my letter. Thank
   you very much!
   Suddenly she's tired. She's just lain down when she grabs
a book from the bedside table, as always. Dietmar Brandtner:

short and sweet. Over seventy haikus, one for every year. She throws it back onto the pile.

*

He actually does call back.
– It took a while for me to find the letter with your number.
– Better?
– Better?
– Are you in a better mood now?
– Mine? She exhales.
– And you, have you brushed your teeth?
– I had a late night yesterday.
– Did you have a visitor?
– Don't be so direct.
– I thought I was just showing some polite interest.
– I watched films, alone, like every evening. And you?
– Who was the woman?
– I would have noticed.
– The woman from before, on the phone.
– That wasn't a woman. That was Annegret. She helps me.
– With what?
– I've already written to you about how I'm currently not available for interviews, so please stop with the questions.
– I'd like to meet you.
– That's impossible.
– I have to speak with you personally.
– Beware!

*

Two weeks ago she'd written to him asking for an interview. Please send me a photograph, one likes to know with whom one is dealing with, he replied. She felt – and she's embarrassed to think of it now – flattered, because she assumed that the request was an expression of his personal interest in her, and she posted the required photograph on the same day. She quickly regretted it. He'd changed his mind, he wrote, and would not be available for interviews for the foreseeable future. After she recovered as best she could from the heavy blow, at least until her lip stopped wobbling, she reached for the phone.

***

She claps down the sun-visor and accelerates. Wherever she looks she can see tree-cutters at work: here, standing on their ladders, and there, the crippled bushes and trees they've left behind. There's still frost on the fields, but the ground will soon give way under the heavy soles of the farmer standing in the middle of the field, who'll go home with mud caked on his shoes. She beeps until he moves his gaze from the sky and turns around; waving, she speeds past him. She sees him looking after her in the back mirror.

*

– What attracts you to living out here?
– I live in here. He gets up, refills his glass and looks around his room.
– Do you know your neighbours?
– You're the first critic I've allowed inside.
– I'm not a critic.

- Critics are a bunch of sinners. Every one of them has written a novel, which he happens to have on him just so he can force it on me.
- I already have a publisher, thank you.
- Well then, bravo. Just like I said. Where are your works published?
- I'm asking the questions.
- My neighbours, no, I don't have any, I don't know any.
- I saw one on the drive here and I said hello.
- What do you want to talk about?
- You. Let's start with your most recent poems.
- Beware!
- Is that your favourite word?
  He falls silent.

*

She's been waiting for thirty-two minutes. He said he needed to go to the bathroom. Then, behind thick rounded glass, the grandfather clock had struck the half hour. Now it was two minutes past the hour. *I've got to go*, she'd written the sentence down and, meanwhile, she coloured in the letters, making them bulky. From the sofa she takes yet another look around the room. The room reveals nothing about him. The furniture looks as though it has somehow wandered in by chance, with no one there to tell its history. There are no picures, apart from a dusty Asiatic symbol, which hangs on a nail, unframed, next to the grandfather clock, at about the eye level of a ten year old. The bookcase meets her expectations. She gets up from the sofa in order to examine it more closely. Row after row, her gaze flits across the spines. Yes, they're all there, the Greats, and yes, the 'youngest' book is around forty years old. The books could all easily pass at a small town community library in the 1970s.

*

– What are you reading at the moment?
– Nothing. I watch films.
– You're not reading anything?
– Nothing of consequence.
– That makes me curious! Cook books?
– No. I jump from one to the other in order to stimulate my appetite. In this respect your question about the cookbooks isn't bad. But I still lack any appetite.
– You're not hungry?
– Not in the least, no.

*

She points at the symbol. – Is it Japanese?
– Yes.
– What does it mean?
– No idea.
– You lived for a long time in Japan.
– No, no, I went there a few times, but not for long. Long time ago now.
– Why did you hang it there?
– Did I? I don't know. I can ask Annegret.
– No thanks, no need.

*

– We're not getting anywhere.

– No.

– Where were you for such a long time?

– I made notes for myself.

– Are you writing in another room?

– Only because you're here. I can't write if I'm not alone.

– I thought you went to the toilet.

– I did.

*

– Where do you get sustenance?

– Sustenance for what – for being human? A man? A patient?

– An artist.

– I've used everything up.

– Your late work is evidence to the contrary.

– Late work? I write haikus because I have nothing else to say and wanted to have fun with these *petits riens*. Trifles, he translates in passing. – Vanities! My work is as it stands, I completed it with *Behind the Mountain*. We can talk about that, but not about my waning body, my waning poetry. Allow me my daily faux-Japanese happiness! Now he even addressed her with the familiar '*du*' though he had not meant to.

She ignores it.

– You write a haiku every day?

He nods. He looks tired. Silence. She looks at her watch, almost half a minute. Then he says, like a schoolboy conjugating his verbs – *Nulla dies sine linea*. No day without ...

– I do understand. Have you written one today?

He nods. – It goes, wait a sec, it goes like this:

Into empty air
I bravely grasp with both hands
that are emptier still

She looks at him: – You are creating something out of nothing.
– That's it! He smiles. – Please, you have to leave now.
– It's just getting…
– Please.

He goes to the door and holds it open.
– You refuse everything.

He pales. – You misunderstand. Come again tomorrow if you like. I'll ask Annegret to prepare lunch.

She tidies the notebook away and puts the pen in the bag and stands up.

He's suddenly full of life again. – By the way, I saw a wonderful film yesterday. Perhaps you know—
– No, definitely not.

She takes her jacket and leaves.

*

This peculiar smell is still playing around her nose. She winds down the window. When she walked past him, a real shower of smell landed on her: it was like he had scent glands with motion-sensors in his temples, which sprayed every time a person came too close. She tries to catch hold of this smell, but it teases her: it's there and at the same time it escapes her. The draught doesn't affect it. It dances around her nose, strokes her gums, tickles the nape of her neck: yes, dusty, and a little rancid, like rye-flour perhaps, but more intense, far more intense.

***

She dreamt of his mouth. He spoke, *look, it's me!* She didn't recognise him. He bared his teeth: *well, do you recognise me now?* Yes, but she said *no*. He played with his tongue, sticking it in and out of his mouth at a dizzying speed. *Brandtner, you're a pig*, she said, and then his mouth laughed like the robber *Hotzenplotz*.

*

On the way, she looks out for the farmer from the previous day with no success. She beeps anyway as she drives past his field.

*

Brandtner is wearing a clean shirt and has combed his hair.

*

- I'd like to go back and talk about this issue of hunger. You said yesterday you didn't have any.
- That's right. I like to play with my cutlery and let the food dance and play on my tongue. I spit it out once it loses its flavour. I lose interest quickly. It was different before, in some respects.
- The ragout is delicious.
- I'll let Annegret know.
- Does watching other people eat give you pleasure?
- I was just thinking about that. Yes, sure, yes, it's entertaining for me, and you look rather cheerful when you eat.
- Really?
- Now I've spoilt your appetite.

– You have. Have you written your poems today?

– No.

She quotes him: – *Nulla dies sine linea*.

He waves it away with his hand. – *Nulla regula sine exceptione* works just as well. By the way, my favourite dishes are very simple, the seemingly banal, which only gives my tongue an aftertaste, if you follow me.

– Not really. Although, a good haiku is similar. Play with me, it demands of you, make something of me, give me an aftertaste.

– Of me? That's critic's jargon. You mean the reader.

– Do you write strictly to the five-seven-five structure?

– I saw an interesting film yesterday, perhaps you know it? A classic! *Rabid – The Roaring Death*.

– Sorry, no. What has the film got to do with haikus?

– Nothing. You don't know it? It's a horror film.

– Could we stick to the subject for a moment? So, you write every haiku with five, seven and five syllables?

He sighs. – Yes.

There's a silence.

– Mr Brandtner, please talk to me!

He seems bored. – That's the fun of it. Haiku means as much or as little as comic verse. That's what it's about, even the *Jisei*, the death poem, (again the running translation!), you understand, contains a joke. A little form filled with a little joke.

Without wanting to, he starts to pick up speed. – Do you know Hubbell? There is a splendid *Jisei* by him, which I wish I could say was mine:

Having spent my life
In the service of beauty
Now human garbage.

He beams at her. – So?
– And the joke?
– And the joke!? Come on now, don't tell me you don't get it?

*

They have left the kitchen and are now, like the day before, sitting in the room opposite; her on the sofa, him in his armchair.

*

– How's your libido?
– What do you want from me?
– An answer.

He looks to the ceiling. Then he whispers in a low voice. – I'd like to know what you look like from the inside!
– Excuse me?
– It was a quote.
– From? Remind me—
– *Roaring Death*? No.
– It sounds like a horror film.
  He nods.
– I assume it comes from a blood-thirsty murderer.
– Exactly. He whispers – I'd like to turn your insides out and look at them closely!
– What's your libido like?

- We already had that question. Next!
- That wasn't really a quote from the roaring horror film?
- No.
- Then what?
- I've forgotten. But do you remember the scene where, suddenly, out of a tender white armpit, a phallic spike comes bursting out? Oh, right, you haven't seen it. It's a young woman who grows this spike, interestingly.
- Back to the topic at hand. Sexuality.
- I'm on the topic!
- *You* are the topic, not some horror film. It's striking that your poetry always deals with the flesh.
- That's true.

I see my own flesh
Faithless, rotting from the bone
There, Death is at work.
There you have your answer.

*

He enters the room again, after he's just been out for a short while. His face looks freshly washed.

*

- Why do you greet my neighbours?
  She looks at him, not understanding.
- Yesterday, you said you greeted my neighbour. Why did you do that?
- Now! The farmer! Yes, I greeted him. But I can't tell you why.

– Then I'll tell you: to claim closeness. You're doing it the whole time! You think it's enough to create intimacy by feigning interest. An honest conversation can never take place, at least not between us. Because nothing comes from nothing.

– It's my job to ask questions.

– That's no excuse! It's my job to arrange words into lines. I still have to take responsibility for every line I write.

– Really? I'd like to talk about that.

– You're avoiding the issue. Now I'm asking the questions. Where do you draw your strength from?

– My work as a journalist.

– What do you live for?

– My freedom. I answer only to my conscience and that which I call truth.

– Well remembered! And you write. What?

– Prose.

– Why do you write?

– Because I must.

– And now I'll repeat my question: what do you want from me?

– I wanted to get to know you. I've always wanted to.

– You bore me. I'm not finished with you yet. Come again tomorrow.

*

She drives directly into the glare of the sun, squinting. Tears run down her face and tickle her. She wipes them away angrily. You stupid, stinking bastard. She sniffs the snot back into her nose and whimpers. Where is his scent now? Is he already so familiar to her that she can no longer sense it? During the conversation, it came flying at her from time to time, settled on her clothing, clung to her skin, but now it's gone.

***

He greets her straightaway at the door. – I'm sorry, he says, I'm in a bad mood. Tired.
– Too many horror films yesterday?
– Yes, probably. I slept badly. Go ahead, I'll follow directly.

*

She can't believe her eyes. Her photo hangs on the wall, stuck on with blue-tack, between the grandfather clock and the Japanese symbol, but higher, around the same level as his eyes when he's standing. The photo she sent him!

*

He sits. – Do you feel like taking your clothes off?
– Not right now, no.
She wonders how she was able to put together an answer, however stutteringly. He looks at her; she looks at her photo.
– Where shall we stop it?
She shrugs. – Let's listen to it. She starts her voice recorder. *What attracts you to living out here? I live in here...*
Together they listen to the discussion of the past two days. He folds his arms and stares at the floor. She pretends to write hurried notes, although she is only drawing an awkward stick-girl. At the same time, she tries to observe him.
I wanted to get to know you. I've always wanted to.
You bore me. I'm not finished with you. Come again tomorrow.

She turns the machine off and puts it away.

– Something occurred to me yesterday, after you'd left. You remind me of someone.

– Yes, my mother.

– Do I know your mother?

– You don't remember her.

– Perhaps I do.

– You slept with her a couple of times, nothing more. You didn't recognise her afterwards.

– When was that?

– In the 70s.

– Oh. A long time ago. But don't try telling me now, you're my daughter!

Try telling, she jots it down next to the stick-girl. She stares at the words.

– I think I would like to go now. She stands up. – I have enough material, it will do. I'll send it to you to proofread.

– My Goodness! Please sit yourself down again! My bodily destruction continues, not gradually and unnoticeably, but in small, neat, perceptible steps which I see and feel every day. Horrible. So please don't blame me if my memory is crumbling too.

– What are you talking about? You didn't recognise my mother when I was five years old. Men just live for the present, she says. – Goodbye.

– But Annegret is counting on you staying for lunch. And, please, could I add something to the record? Haiku and horror!

It sounds like he's giving a quick summing-up.

– Maybe I'll use it as my title. Thanks. But maybe not.

– Let's talk about it over lunch. He looks at her. – And I'd like to tell you something else. Please.

*

– Taste good?
– Yes, but I'm not hungry.
– It's been a long time since I've had a visitor you know. Yesterday, after you'd left, I looked at the photo and I wished you would come again, turn the lights off and pounce on me, over there on the sofa. Or on my desk. In the pantry. Or the cellar. In the dark, your naked body illuminated by torches I hold in my hands and control. My body, un-observed, would run like a newly serviced machine. And you'd be the mechanic. I find it hard to get rid of these images. It always ends up being physical, doesn't it? He hits his chest. – We write and write against it, but we can't overcome it. When I wrote my first novel, which centred on my strange pubescent body, I turned to the world of my other, spiritualised self, at least a little, and what a happy time it was! Now I'm back again with myself, this strange degenerating body. So it is. The way of all earthly things.
– You only talk about yourself.
– Yes, awful. I wanted to express it quite differently. Can I try again?
– Last chance.
– *Look in the mirror*
  Me and you stand together
  We can't get closer.
– Thanks for lunch.
– Thanks for the visit.

Her Shoes

Inspired by *The Waitress*,
a fragment by Robert Walser.

Smiling was something I learnt. When I ask myself what's changed over the past year, how I've moved up life's ladder, I can answer with that single word: smiling. If, today – as you might do on birthdays and New Year's Eve, those two dates when you treat yourself with a little more kindness than usual – I were to examine myself, today, in the middle of the year, on a day which has no special meaning for me, which reminds me of nothing that I can't forget or shouldn't forget, if I were to stand in front of the mirror, look deep into my eyes and let the past year run through my mind, I can say that word *smile* to my face. I've learnt to smile, and this word alone should prove to me that it's possible to move up in life. Of course. Who would have thought, a year ago, that I could possess such an ability just a few hundred days later. Oh what a surprise, oh wonderful, unfathomable, beautiful ladder of progress.

She taught me it. She began to practice with me from the first day. From the moment I said 'Hello' and my name; from the moment she looked at my feet and said, 'Girl, surely not in those' as she smiled, naturally. Her smile is a double line of contentment (bottom lip) and satisfaction (top lip) over which her iron will extends, yet remains hidden. Smiling, she handed me the comfy shoes in which I should, according to her, step up to my work. Smiling, she explained in broad terms the working day, the filing system, the hygiene standards, the bar taps, the coffee machine and the till. Smiling, she watched me take my first steps in her shoes, turn around and hesitantly return her smile. "Not so nervously," she said, again and again she said it, until she said nothing at all and we just smiled at each other. I'd succeeded, finally.

*

Today is Thursday, which is just as unimportant as the fact that I've been working here for fourteen months; just as unimportant as my name, her name, the question of what I plan to do when I get off and whether he'll pick me up or not, like he said he would.

The last customer has piled his loose change in high copper towers on the bar. With the last coin, he taps his drunken beat on the lacquered wood while staring at his shoes.

'Come, come here to me.'

She holds two tiny glasses in her hands, turning them slowly on their thin stems. I sit on a stool, legs wide apart, and draw my glass towards me. 'To life,' she says and, gripping the bar with her left hand, throws her head back and turns the glass bottom up with her right.

The sharp cognac laps over my gums. I swirl it around in my mouth with my tongue before I swallow. 'Tired?' I nod. 'Another.' She refills. 'How much is it, love?' I say. She smiles her smile and sways her head meaningfully from side to side. The last customer knocks hard and monstrously, he keeps knocking. We listen to him for a while. 'The gentleman would like to pay,' I say. She gives me a sign, *Leave it be.*

You can find the Last Customer, anywhere, anytime; and you'll also find the Regular. When the door closes behind him, you know who you're dealing with immediately, without a doubt. The lack of greeting (*they know me here*); his look, which DOES NOT sweep across the room as he steers towards his seat; the way in which he throws his car keys on the table before he sits: all these are unmistakeable signs. Straightaway, you accept him for what he is: the Regular. Straightaway it's as though he's never been away, as if he's as necessary to this small world as the bar or the till, without which the pub would not be a pub. The Regular focuses his strength. Easy, nonchalant and relaxed, he enters the world from which he is descended.

You can find the Last Customer anywhere and you can find the Regular, just like you can here tonight. As she fills the tiny glasses for the third time with a practised hand, the door opens and he enters. He does not greet us or bother to look up; he throws the keys on the table, falls into his seat and makes his demands: to be served without delay, and graciously, in accordance with his status, his name. 'Espresso Grappa.' He arrives later every night on purpose, every night a little later, a little nearer to closing time. 'The coffee machine has just been cleaned,' I say. 'Sorry,' I smile the smile, which she has taught me.

He grabs my wrist quick as a flash and presses hard. 'Careful,' he hisses. He lets go, throwing my wrist to one side, a dismissive movement. *And now hop to it*, he waves his hand in the direction of the bar. 'Go.' I suppress the worst curses and set off to look behind the bar for an axe.

*

She's there, standing and waiting for me with a guarded expression. She looks me in the eye, serious and calm, but I can detect her anxiety; I can see her fear and I feel as though I've been betrayed. The yellow-tinged hair-piece, which she fixes to her forehead every day with hairspray, may conceal the worry-furrows and sorrow-crevices, the woe-grooves and lonely-scratches of her skin, but it can't conceal the fear in her eyes.

I tear my gaze away from hers, push past her towards the kitchen and hear her footsteps following me. She stands close; I hear her breath on my neck. 'I'm going to kill him,' I say, stumbling a few steps forwards, sidewards, 'I'm going to kill him.' She hugs me from behind. I sink my head and struggle against the sobs stumbling up my throat. She places her cheek between my shoulder-blades. 'For God's sake,' she says, 'what's wrong with you?' I struggle to breathe and at the moment when my tears are about to fall, she hits me hard with her fist in the hollow of my back, which is still warm from her cheek. 'Pull yourself together.' My hate jumps from him to her in an instant. I want to hit her, to shake her, collide violently into her body. I hear her leave the kitchen; I hear her footsteps on the wooden floor behind the bar; I hear the hiss of the coffee machine, shocked out of its night-time rest, hear the machine's gargling and humming, the rattle of the cup against the metal under the piston as it is filled; finally I hear the 'pfff', with which the machine recovers. I hear a spoon ring, hear the squeaking of the glass-bottom on the shelf, the knock as the neck of the bottle hits the Schnapps glass and the glug of the Grappa in the glass. With renewed determination I step out of the kitchen and behind the bar, take the little tray from her, see her smile, the smile she has taught me, suppress the hate released by this smile, like a little burp rising from my stomach, turn away and carry the tray to his table. 'Enjoy,' I say, *die,* I think, as I put the tray down on the imitation-marble. And I smile the smile she has taught me.

I stand there in her shoes, with her smile on my lips. She stands there and lets herself be smiled at by me. 'Are you getting picked up today?' I put my head to one side and twitch my left shoulder. It can mean yes or no or I won't say or I don't know. She doesn't ask. She says, 'He seems nice.' He. My heart twitches just as easily as my shoulder. Him, more than one. Maybe she means him? Or maybe that him, or this him. He seems nice, she said. Maybe him? In the mirror behind the glasses I direct her smile towards myself and imagine him in a row between predecessors and successors. He seems nice. The man standing in a row on which the smell of a successor already lingers and wafts towards me. He seems nice: the man who reminds me of the future. Of a future with other, similar men. And me. The same endless game, another man's name, a new man's face, a new man's smell, and the brief hope, that feeling above the feeling that something will happen, will jump into motion. The feeling under the feeling knows better, knows what's coming, knows what it means and what it does NOT mean. The feeling under the feeling does not let itself be so easily, so readily distracted. The feeling under the feeling is disgust. The disgust disappears in an instant, and then it's non-detectable, deflected, distracted, a flexible arrow, a boomerang. Although it's quick to vanish out of sight, undetectable, it will return, this bent baton, refreshed from its outing and stronger than before. It settles down, thick, hard, firm, in the middle of the nest of the heart. It settles down at the heart's inn, freely and without shame, a Regular. Greetings not necessary: they know me here.

'He seems nice,' she says and brushes a strand of hair behind my ear. 'Him?' I joke, nodding at the Last Customer. 'Or him?' I gesture towards the Regular, who's playing with his keyring, looking as though he's waiting for something. She laughs. She takes off her smile and laughs quickly. 'No,' she says, 'him,' and points to the door, behind which the world lies. 'You've got to learn to differentiate,' she says. 'It's got nothing to do with you. These poor fools, what have they got to do with you?'

The Pit

Standing in the main hall of the station, her head thrown back, she goes through the train connections on the departures board while mumbling to herself. *I'll take that one. The ten fifty eight. Eight minutes to go. Buy tickets? Have a smoke?*

With a lit cigarette, she walks up and down the platform, rubbing her legs together between each step as if she were freezing. Another woman stops close by and looks over in her direction. *I've got to stand over there to smoke, I know, in that yellow square on the platform, but as you see I'm not doing that. So what are you going to do? Do something!* The woman shakes her head and walks on. *A madwoman,* she says, the words fading as she walks away. *A madwoman! Like I give damn! A madwoman: how true!*

*

She sits in a window seat in the open-plan carriage and, in the window, she looks into her eyes. *I shouldn't smoke. I shouldn't drink. I should lose weight. I should exercise, at my age. I should avoid stress. I shouldn't complain so much,* she murmurs.

A female voice comes through on the loudspeaker, wishing the passengers *a warm welcome* and requesting they show each other *good will*, since the reservation system is not working due to a technical error.

Good will! She looks around, counts only three fellow passengers, equally dispersed as if a spirit of orderliness had sat each of them down that way, and laughs loudly. Another passenger looks at her testily. Then he gives a weak smile, opens a book and begins to read with utmost concentration. The other two seem to be deaf. A woman has been looking in her handbag for something for a while; a boy energetically presses the buttons of his mobile communication and entertainment device, staring fixedly at the screen.

She turns to face her reflection in the dark window again, nods in greeting, and confirms to herself: *A madwoman*. This time the words don't fade away in the wind. The passenger with the book clears his throat repeatedly with an ever-increasing volume without breaking his concentration. She watches his pupils glide from left to right, to left, to right. She envies him. She takes the rucksack down from the overhead storage, undoes it and examines its contents.

Another announcement: the same voice. She recommends passengers visit the On-Board Bistro; however, the refrigerator has broken down, the selection is therefore limited.

A warm beer. Why not? She turns away from her reflection, stands up, picks up the rucksack, wishes her three fellow passengers a good evening and goes on her way. The man with the book quickly mumbles something incomprehensible. She answers without turning around as she walks: *Thank you. Very kind of you. You too.*

This Monday night there's hardly anyone on the train. She walks rather briskly for her age and weight against the direction of travel, sometimes colliding painfully against the seats and armrests, until she reaches the last carriage. *Wrong way. You can't go on. Turn right round and go back!*

On her return, she recognises the faces of the passengers as if they belonged to old acquaintances: people she had something to do with a long time ago, and she has to stop herself from repeatedly asking, *Please help me – when was it? Where? And what was your name again?* The three passengers in her carriage also awaken vague thoughts and memories in her which she cannot place. The man with the book – of course, she knows him – but from where? And the woman who's still looking for something in her handbag, she knows her for sure – and the young man, who so nimbly moves the pad of his thumb across the keyboard of his device. She stands still and looks at each of them in turn. But none of them seem to remember her. Someone taps her shoulder from behind. She turns around; a woman in a blue uniform stands in front of her. *The woman from the announcements!* The uniform nods.

She points in the direction of travel: *Is this the way to the On-Board Bistro?*

The uniform nods.

I don't have a ticket.

The uniform shakes her head and explains that her colleague is responsible for that and that he's usually sitting in the On-Board Bistro. Her voice is brighter than over the tannoy.

*

She sits in front of a bottle of red wine and a piece of paper. The young man didn't want to pour any un-chilled beer for her at the bar. It didn't come out of the tap properly and tasted horrible. The conductor, who held an empty beer glass in his hand, nodded in agreement. When she asked for a ticket, and he asked for the destination of her journey, she thought about it for a long time, even though she knew the answer. *Fog.* He looked at her as if she'd said Chongquing. *Fog in the Amrum language.* Again: the look. He could issue her a ticket as far as Hamburg; she wouldn't get any further tonight anyway. She draws a couple of flowers in the margins of the paper. The same ones she draws at every audition, at every telephone conversation, in every discussion. 'I'm going,' she'd written, 'through the backdoor, otherwise I won't be able to leave. I'm travelling by night and if I reach Fog tomorrow at around noon, I'll stay another night there, and then I'll leave a second time, this time for good. That's the plan so far. This letter is too late, I know. I might as well have left it on the table at home and then gone out. You see, Stefan, in this undertaking, I'm lacking a director who can organise my drifting. It'll be immediately clear to you that I've left my medication and mobile phone behind. I'm travelling without baggage.' Right at the bottom of the page she'd already signed: 'Yours Ulli.' She didn't get any further. But the number of flowers increased. She poured herself a full glass. She turned the empty bottle upside down on the table, until the last drops ran onto the white tablecloth, rolled the paper into a cigar and stuck it into the bottle. *Message in a bottle.*

And now? It's cold. On the station forecourt the wind blows towards her. She presses her lips tightly together in order to keep hold of the cigarette. On the other side of the street is the theatre. She inhales deeply, holds her breath briefly and presses the smoke out. But the wind is so strong that she can't see the smoke, so she feels no satisfaction. She shelters in a corner of the station entrance and watches the smoke dissolve. From this corner, the theatre's presence can only be sensed. She feels nothing. She puckers her lips, blows the smoke out and follows it with her eyes. After she's stamped out the stub with her heel, she crosses the road. She hesitates. She hardly dares to walk around the theatre; she walks with her head hanging low, as if the building is watching her, as if she's scared the walls might talk and interrogate her.

Without thinking she turns right at the stage entrance, walks to the end of the street and turns right again, until she's standing in front of *The Living Room*. It's still open. She hears voices, a racket, and music. In no other place has she spent more nights of her life in the company of equals. When the canteens closed, you had to move on to the *The Living Room*. She nods, just as she nodded to her reflection in the train window: nods in greeting, an expression of solidarity, before carrying on for around three blocks until she reaches *Uschi's Pub*, where she always went to be alone. But *Uschi's Pub* no longer exists. The fence in front of the entrance is still there, but locked up. The neon signs have already been removed and have left black rims on the facade where bare electric cables hang freely. *What's going on? Uschi! You can't just disappear! It's just not done.* She turns away, lights a cigarette and walks on.

She doesn't have a watch on her. She never wears a watch, in recent years her mobile always showed the time when she needed it. How long has she walked for? Two hours? Then it should be around three in the morning. It's quiet in the house. She reads the name on the postbox with the help of her lighter. *A and H Cordes.* She nods in agreement. She knows where the keys are; she herself decided on their hiding place when she – Albert was a PhD student and Hannah was still little – regularly left her bag in the cloakroom and found herself standing in front of a locked door at night. Back then, the house looked the same at this time of night as it did now. She bends down, turns the stone and finds it. *Thanks, Albert, but I'm afraid I can't accept your invitation. Seriously now, I know you didn't put it there for me. You were so sure I wouldn't come back, so sure, that you didn't even look for a new hiding place, right? You were right. All the best. I'm off again.* She steps a few metres back, stands still and thinks.

She sits at her old writing desk, opens the drawer and, as expected, finds a block of paper, tears off a sheet and places it in front of her. A tea light is enough to recognise her own writing. 'Hannah, I'm just travelling through. My train doesn't leave until half-six. I wandered around and I've arrived here without having planned it. The key was under the stone. I'm interrupting your life for the last time, uninvited, I know, and I ask you to forgive me for saying a few things to you, which I always forgot to say when we saw each other. My life has rushed past me. My strengths have long diminished and I haven't really done anything to keep them up. For some time now I've observed how my mental strength has been quietly bidding farewell. I can't remember anything new and my memories are fading as well. Not a single line of text. Over the last few weeks I've been rehearsing *Richard II*. I desperately wanted this role for years; why, I couldn't say, and now that I can't do it anymore, I have to perform it. Why Richard? I hear you ask and your tone reveals what you think of it. Do you remember when I played Hamlet, my first male role? Of course you remember. You were twelve. You told me after the dress rehearsal that you were ashamed of me. Today

I'm the one who is ashamed. At rehearsals, I stand on stage and can't speak, not a single sentence, because the text, which I try to bludgeon into my brain every night, is simply gone, vanished, erased. I stand completely still and stare into the void. I want the ground to swallow me whole. Even falling through the stage trapdoor seems like a way out. Twelve metres, after all! I'd have to be prepared for broken bones in any case, and internal bleeding couldn't be avoided from that height. 'Then do it,' you used to say. 'Just do it!' You're right. 'What do your imaginary worlds have to do with my life, Mum?' you asked. Fear, Hannah, it's there; it feasts on me, and when I listen to my inner voice, I can only hear the smacking of its lips. I did something this evening that I never believed I could do: for the first time in forty years, I simply didn't turn up. I sat by the *Landwehr* canal. Then I drove to the station and took the last train. I'm on the way to the island.

On re-reading this letter, it's clear I'm just talking about myself again. Forgive me.

P.S. I'm glad that my old writing desk is still here. I hope that you're happy, eternal little daughter, at your father's side. If not, then I advise you urgently, immediately to start your own household.

She doesn't know how to end it. The 'M' is already there so she puts the point of the ball-pen on it and circles it until it becomes a small, black spot – nothing more.

She tears off another piece of paper and quickly writes:

'Dear Albert, I wanted to write a letter to you too, but time passed quickly. I have to go before you or Hannah wake up and find me here at the desk. I'll put the keys under the stone again. Ulli.' She folds the two letters in half, writes Hannah on one and Albert on the other, but when she's about to stand up, something happens. She unfolds Hannah's letter again and writes underneath: 'I just remembered a line, a single line from *Richard*: "Thus play I in one person many people/And none contented." Yes, I was many and always the same; to be dull was unbearable to me. And three roles later it was still the same. And after a year – a Penthesilea, a Titania, a Caecilia, a Mary Stuart later – it was still the same. And so on. For forty years. Forty years! Up to this day. I was interviewed recently. The journalist reminded me of you. She had a way of indicating in the question what she thought of the answer. "Is it particularly difficult for an actor to grow old?" "No idea, I was always an actor, so I can't make any comparison." A stupid answer, I know. But I can't forget the question.'

She sits in the train heading towards Husum. She's nodded off. She jolts awake when the train stops. She feels as though she's taken sleeping pills and has a dry mouth; her tongue sticks thick and heavy to her gums. *Have we stopped for a long time?* The man opposite smiles and says no. The conductor's just been and gone, the signal's red but no one knows why, so they just have to wait, he explains. *I have to get my connection. Are you in a hurry*, he asks. *No*, she says. And: *yes,* she says then.

When she changes trains in Husum, her knees hurt and she can only get up from her seat with great effort, and it's only with help from the conductor, who supports her on one side, that she manages the two steps from the train to the platform. *Take your time*, he says, but she turns away without thanking him and quickens her pace.

On the short journey to Niebüll, she puts her legs up. *Gran – you tired?* Asks a boy, perhaps sixteen years old, as he passes. *I wouldn't know where to start, my boy.* He turns to her and quickly shows her the finger. In Niebüll, she's even got time to get a coffee and smoke a cigarette, and after that she feels fairly alright and can ignore her pains.

When she gets off at Niebüll, the smell of dead fish and wet seagull droppings wafts towards her and she raises her hand in greeting. *Here I am.* Arriving on the ferry, she inhales deeply as if smoking the biggest and most valuable cigarette of all time. And it tastes good. She sits down on the deck in the open air. Soon, the wind blows so cold under her coat that she goes inside and orders breakfast at the ferry's restaurant. The waitress lays the table. *Can I ask you something?* The waitress says yes with a hoarse voice and smiles, so that her yellowish teeth and exposed fillings are visible. *Do you have a pen and paper?* The waitress shows her little order book. She can remember everything anyway, she says, pointing at her forehead and puts the book and pen down next to the folded napkin.

She tries to make her handwriting as small as possible.

'Dear Journalist,

You asked me a question.

Is it particularly difficult for an actor to grow old? Today, I'll answer. A stradivarius might, in the coming years, become better. But a body, which is always growing fatter, which can no longer do somersaults – I can't even express some things any more, even if I wanted to. Had I known that, I would never have become an actor. Added to that is forgetfulness, which I'd so wished for before now. My forgetfulness. I can't remember anything anymore.

As a young woman, I thought I put one over on life by choosing a career where I could play anything, any time. Men and monsters, children and murderers, victims and playboys, kings and slaves, fraudsters and believers. Life, time, could have nothing on me. I would turn the plan life had for me, like it has for every other person, on its head, change it as I wanted, wind it forwards and back, mix it all together. How I endlessly pitied the dancers! It was over by thirty, they said. Some cheated until forty, but they didn't get any success or self-satisfaction from it and it still ended in shame and loneliness. The actors, by contrast – me included – could perform as long as they still drew breath. Life and career complimented each other. So long as you had one, you had the other. Retirement? A joke! Pension? Paralysis! Actors don't retire. Never. They remain in the world, they take on any challenge. They bear the pain when they learn they must lose a loved-one; they don't allow any illness to bring them to their knees. The show must go on: on the same morning as an operation under general anaesthetic, or with fever, or a shattered knee, diarrhoea, torn muscles, dizziness, heart palpitations. With numb limbs, claustrophobia, sweats. Modern medicine is one's best friend. The only personal contacts I usually have after two years living in a new city are a couple of culturally-interested doctors: in most cases, an orthopaedic and a surgeon.

Twelve years ago, when I was fifty, I had a heart attack. At fifty! As a woman! It would never have occurred to me. I didn't notice it: nothing more than a period of deep tiredness and general weakness. I thought it was depression. At a *general check-up* my doctor-friend found scars on my heart. I laughed because it didn't surprise me. *A scarred heart suits me*. He didn't laugh. *It's serious*, he said. Probably my heart didn't get enough nutrition for years. *Oh yes, that's right!* He looked sad. He meant the blood and oxygen supply. One could therefore assume that my coronary artery had, for years, narrowed irreversibly.

Throughout my life, the fear of acting and the fear of not acting have been equal, more or less. Of course, there were moments of unbalance almost every day. Of course, they tortured me, both of these fears, and since they weighed hundreds of kilos it was very painful, but through their simultaneous presence they balanced each other out, reined each other in. Now the fear of no longer being able to act is setting in. I've become forgetful. My narrow heart vessels don't just starve my heart, they also shrink my memory. My doctor has already confirmed that after just five years a noticeable reduction in the power of memory may occur. It's been fifteen years for me. I never really cared about it, no, never came to terms with it: I just ignored it. As long as I could. I could remember everything: it's always been like that. All the birthdays and the names of all the children, with whom I, myself a child, had ever been befriended, and the names of all the siblings of these children as well as their phone numbers. All the passwords, usernames and access data I'd ever entered. All the secrets ever confided to me. All the meals I'd ever eaten; places I'd searched for; words I'd heard. And of course the many thousands of lines I'd recited during my career on the stage. I worked on the technique of learning-by-heart and I trained daily. Until, after a few years in the job, I began to suffer from all these lines that had nothing to do with me. I did not have the technique of forgetting the texts! All the rituals I thought of fell flat: the masses of text would not let themselves be disposed of. There was no rubbish tip where I could dump them; no toilet I could vomit into, no paper I could wrap them up in. They seemed to slumber in some remote corner, always ready to push to the front at an untimely hour. Those stage swines. They kept their hold on me as stubbornly as the fat deposits in my veins and just as irreversible – so it seemed to me, until I began to forget. I forgot uncontrollably: piece by piece, phrase by phrase, word by word, dialogue by dialogue. What was left were single lines, which I could no longer file away, no longer connect with anything. *Who is speaking?* I often ask, *hello, who's speaking? And what are you speaking about? What's the topic? Who are you talking to and what is your desire, your sorrow, your intention?* A wasteland of text, a tattered cloth of tattered text remains. More holes than fabric. As if someone had pointed a machine gun at it and shot all his ammunition.

That's how I seem to be right now. I've written seventeen little pages full, both front and back. Meanwhile I've forgotten your question.'

She gets the message-in-a-bottle out of her rucksack and pulls the letter for her partner out. She reads it over again, can't remember how all the small flowers came to be there, and tears it up. She manages to roll up the seventeen pages into a bundle and put it into the neck of the bottle instead. *Stefan.* Her voice is hoarse; she clears her throat. *Stefan. I can't remember now what I wanted to tell you. But I still have time.* The waitress has come to her table and looks at her questioningly. *Excuse me I was just mumbling to myself. But since you're here I'd like another coffee. And can I smoke?*

On the pier in Wittdün she watches pairs of oystercatchers with open red beaks skydiving and wonders whether the sound they're making is a screech or a whoop of joy. She focuses on the sound and then tries to imitate it, for which she earns some head-shaking from a group of young mothers with prams. *More of a joyful whooping,* she decides and smiles happily at the young mothers. She gets on behind them on the bus, which drives past the lighthouse and through the beech grove before stopping at the Rehab Clinic where the mothers with all their prams get out. She remains alone with the driver and calls to him when she'd like to get off.

She's been travelling for thirteen hours. She opens the garden gate where she comments, sullenly as usual: *Far too low!* The door has jammed shut again. She pulls it towards her and kicks it at the same time as she turns the key and curses. She lies down on the bed in her coat and doesn't move anymore. She searches the cupboards above the kitchen counter. She sits by the stove and smokes a cigarette. She massages her swollen knee. She considers whether she should take off her coat. She falls asleep.

Someone is knocking. She starts up. *Yes!* She gets up, goes to the door and opens it. A police officer holds a note in his hand. Mrs Witthagen? Ulrike Witthagen?

Yes.

You were reported missing in Berlin this evening.

Missing? By who?

From a Mr Stefan Rausch. You live together?

Yes, but why missing? I'm here. To work, I'm in the middle of it, I need peace and quiet.

You've got a heart condition and you don't have your vital medication with you, he says.

That's a misunderstanding. I've got my medication with me. I'm fine.

I apologise for bothering you. No harm meant. The heart is no laughing matter.

She thanks the policeman for his efforts and wishes him a good day. He points towards the overcast sky. *It won't get any better today.*

'I think about the shame all the time, Stefan, even though I never talked about it with you,' she writes. She had, after the policeman's visit, stood for a while by the window, smoked a few cigarettes and listened to every sound until her thoughts took her prisoner again. 'I actually believe that shame was my true companion during all these years and through all these plays. If I think back on it, I had the most success with those plays where I felt the most shame. And it's here in this island-home where I've always hidden myself again and again when things weren't going well, when the shame pinned me down and gagged me. A long time ago, just after Hannah's birth, I played Iphigenia. But I lacked drive. I loved like never before. I wanted to be with Hannah. No heart attacks, no pain, no doubt, no drunken stupors threatened my life, or must I say my creativity? Nothing was as strong as this life, which completely satisfied me. During the first days of rehearsal, I just cried and no one understood why. I was love-sick. Then I drank the first cup of coffee, despite my hungry child at home who wanted to be breast-fed. I smoked the first cigarette, drank the first glass of wine. And cried even more since I had a guilty conscience to add to my love-sickness. Albert looked at me sadly whenever I came home. There was no going back. After a few weeks, I began to spend night and day with my role again. Hardly saw my home, sat for days and nights on end on the rehearsal-stage, in the canteen, spent all night long in bars. Mostly alone at a separate table, with a dark, forbidding look to ward off unwanted company, since my role demanded isolation. I was already fat back then. And I was deeply ashamed of my body. And yet, one day at rehearsal, I took off my clothes. It was unbearable. But I stayed as I was. My Iphigenia was naked. I was hot, I was cold, I felt anxious, my heart raced, and everything inside me cried: Go away, just go away! Stop! Lights out! I wanted to disappear. Without fuss. Just to be gone, swallowed by the darkness of the total *Noir* or be pulled up into the fly-loft. Out of shame I cried my eyes out on the open stage, everyday anew, and the tears never lessened, because the repetition did not have any habituating effect on me, did not soothe me. A secret lonely rehearsal took place here at Amrum at night. I took off all my clothes and ran through the heavy rain the whole way over the dunes to the beach, protected by the darkness. Iphigenia does not cry. However the tears were, I sensed, necessary. And now? I play Richard and I die of shame, but it doesn't bring any tears to my eyes. It simply paralyses me. And I have no means of dealing with it. You laughed at me when I told you last week that I just couldn't remember the text. "You've already learnt the whole world literature off by heart," you said, "so a little Richard will fit inside too." No, he doesn't fit. Not a single line. And shame alone isn't enough, because Richard should be able to speak.'

She puts the pen to the side. How long until the sunset? The view outside doesn't give a clue as to the time. It's just as grey as before. There's nothing more to see.

It starts to rain.

The rain beats sidelong against the dark window and drives her out of her armchair. Back and forth she goes to the little kitchen. Three steps forward, three steps back. And suddenly she can see the lines, clearly and within reach, before her:

But whate'er I be,
Nor I nor any man that but man is
With nothing shall be pleased, till he be eased
With being nothing.

She repeats them, hesitant at first and quiet, she tastes the sound, she teases the rhythm, controlling, varying, she breaks it. As she does so, she takes her coat off, slips off her shoes, lets her trousers glide to the floor, tears the socks from her feet, unbuttons her blouse and vest, stands there naked, looks down at herself and ends with: *Being nothing.* She gets the message in the bottle and the spade out of the rucksack and leaves the house.

The rain welcomes her in a cold embrace. She runs quickly against the wind, which wants to force her back towards the dune. The light beam from the lighthouse circles over the island, but does not catch her. *I'm here*, she shouts at it, as if playing games with the lighthouse keeper who keeps trying and failing to catch her with the searchlight. *Here, catch me!* And adds: *I don't mean me, I mean the human inside of me!*

She runs and runs and becomes ever lighter, and the water comes nearer. She can't see it, but she can hear it. She throws the bottle away from her in a high arc, bends down, and begins to dig.

Goldfish Memory

I followed him. Again and again. I was thirteen the first time I did it. In my lunch break, I saw him on the seaside promenade, laughing on the arm of a woman I didn't know. He was pointing at the water when he saw me. For a moment his smile disappeared, he gave me a searching look; but then, as if I'd signalled my complicity, he laughed loudly at something the woman whispered to him and put his arm around her. We walked past each other like strangers. My insides turned cold from my breastbone to my intestines: a powerful internal wintry assault of freezing puddles and black ice.

I counted to ten before following them for a few hundred metres, until he turned around. I stood still and stared at him. He only threw me a quick glance, but it was the deepest, the most long-lasting, that was ever directed towards me. This glance was a sudden, clean cut. A connection lost.

I watched him go, him and this woman; I stood there doing nothing as I watched the strolling couple go like a ship without an anchor, drawing further and further away from the shore.

In the evenings we sat together at the oval table. "Tell us a story," my mother would demand of me. She looked sad. I entertained the family at dinner, because I couldn't bear the silence. They were either very funny or very horrible stories. I made them up – some were basically true and I embellished them. Either a classmate had, in a breath-taking but witty way, been so insolent that the teacher had suffered heart failure, or a classmate's father had rowed out onto the lake in a boat in order to shoot himself at sunset, and I quoted the suicide letter to his daughter. While telling my stories, I would sneak furtive looks at my father. His eyes were completely focused on the food and his ears completely focused on the stories. He ate with a healthy appetite and joined in energetically – laughing or shaking his head sadly according to the kind of reaction the stories demanded from its listeners. Yet we never looked at each other.

I often said my father was dead. But it's not true.

My father drinks. Everyone drinks. *You have to drink a lot* is the most common piece of advice given to me. My father drinks a lot, but never anything hot. He hates hot drinks. He drinks milk if he's thirsty and brandy if he's not. After showering in the morning he puts on his suit. Then he drinks a cup of milk and goes to work. On Saturdays he stays at home and sits in the leather armchair with his suit on. He drinks a glass of brandy at lunch. Then he says: "I have to go back to the office". Most of the time there's an empty seat at dinner, not just on Saturdays. He comes home late in a taxi.

I am nine years old. A few days ago I had my first communion. In church I recited a phrase which I'd learnt by heart in the communion lessons and which, night after night, I'd enthusiastically repeated before going to sleep:

—For my first communion I pray that God my Father and his son protect me and bless me throughout my life.

I had made two separate persons from "God my father" and "my father God"; God, and my father, between whom I had placed a comma in my mind: "For my first communion I pray that God, my father, and his son protect me and bless me throughout my life". My big sister liked it. "Good, I'll do it," she said, "even if I'm not a son." My father said nothing, but he kissed me and nodded when a relative asked if he were proud of me.

I wake up. I can hear a muffled knocking – someone is banging with a hammer on the carpeted floor. I lie there and listen. No. It's my parents; they're fighting. I know what it looks like. Now and again I can hear their suppressed cries. I stay in bed. My sister taught me: if you remain very still and murmur quietly, "I am ready," then Death will grab you, sting you and allow its poison to enter, which instantly spreads and stiffens your body. She's often tried it out when she plays hide and seek or when she doesn't want to be called on at school. It's always worked. She becomes invisible. You just had to remember to shout "let me go" at the right time. "I am ready," I whisper. And already the poison paralyses me. It works!

On Sundays we all dress up nicely and go out in the car. We go on an outing to the pub. There are children's menus and children's desserts. I feel sick. Next to the car park there's a carousel, after which I feel even more sick. Then we get back into the car. My father smokes a cigar. My mother reminds me every time we get in that I should shout "Pull over!" when I'm just about to vomit. It rains often. I press my forehead against the cool window and watch the drops run together.

*

Whether this story is true or not I don't know, but I've heard it so often I can't imagine it's not.

On his thirty-fifth birthday, the 13th of November 1976, my father visited for the first time an illegal casino, which was periodically set up in the hall of a long-established, well-respected hotel. He approached a table, had them explain the rules, didn't quite understand them, and started gambling.

He stumbled into the rainy dawn of Sunday morning clutching to his heart the thickest wallet he himself had ever seen. He'd won all night long, without having understood the rules in much detail.

He wasn't drunk enough to go home yet. The taxi driver pretended not to understand him. "Write the address on this paper," he demanded. "Late-night-bar," jotted my father down. "I don't know it," answered the taxi driver, "come on, I'll take you home. Where do you live?" My father took the wallet out of his jacket, opened it and offered a few notes to the taxi driver. "Late-night-bar," he repeated. It wasn't a bar, but a brothel, though it had an area where drinks were served. There were no other guests, at least none who were drinking. My father ordered a brandy. When he came to, completely soaking wet, he was lying on the sidewalk in front of the establishment. Without his coat, without his watch, without his wallet. His glasses were broken and half hung on his nose, half on his ear. He had a few bloody bruises around his stomach and ribs as well as his face.

He told us the story repeatedly as a warning, I assume, against alcohol, gambling and the red light district, but it wasn't at all effective, either for us children, who found it more exciting, more adventurous than Robinson Crusoe and who loved to hear it again and again and to ask about every detail, nor for my father, who went on drinking, gambling and whoring. He came back by taxi in the early mornings, often badly beaten, injured, tattered, bruised and bleeding, lay down in the bed next to my sister because he knew that my mother – out of concern for the sleeping child – wouldn't interrogate him there, got up in the morning, showered, put on a fresh shirt, a dry-cleaned suit, sucked a eucalyptus mint to hide the smell of alcohol on his breath, and told us the story of his thirty-fifth birthday, which had happened years ago. Although it occurs to me just now that my big sister was never present when my father told the story. She hates my father. She doesn't want him to lie next to her in the bed. My father stinks and he snores. My big sister wakes up and tries to push him out. But my father is heavy and his sleep is as deep as an abyss.

I often dreamt that my father was dead. I woke up screaming because of it, according to witnesses.

I followed him. Again and again. Once, when I was fifteen and working part-time in a cafe belonging to an old married couple, he suddenly was sitting at one of the small marble tables and ordered a glass of milk.

"Please go away!"

"I'd like a glass of milk," he repeated.

The old owner did the rounds and asked the customers whether everything was to their satisfaction.

"And, how's my daughter getting along?"

"You're the father?" The two shake hands. "She could be more polite, particularly to the regulars, but apart from that she's not so bad." The owner bent his head close to my father:

"She's pretty that's the main thing, you know how it is," he adds, winking. My father looks me quickly up and down and nods, appraisingly. At this moment I closed my hand over the handle of a kitchen knife.

"A proper gent, your father," the owner murmured to me. "Can I go home?"

"But of course, and the milk is on the house." Then the two shook hands, as if it gave them the greatest pleasure and they never wanted to stop. I took my chance and went. "Farewell! Mr Storrer, you'll phone me, right?" My father called something incomprehensible after me. I entered the music shop in the building opposite and leafed through a music book while I watched the entrance to the cafe. My father appeared, stood still, looked left, then right, hesitated, and went left up the alleyway.

He doesn't know where he's going. He stops every few metres, examines the window of a pharmacist, a lit-up advert, a menu. At one point he stands there and turns to the passers-by, like a beggar, wordlessly, but with a stupid little smile that asks for sympathy, I can recognise it even from a distance. I'm ashamed. I walk towards him with a few quick steps, grab his sleeve as if I'm about to arrest him, and take him home.

*

Once, years later, we passed each other on the tram. At a stop, I spotted him in a tram going in the opposite direction. People got off and on. He stared in front of him with no expression on his face. He didn't seem to be registering anything. I stared at him through both windows and wondered briefly whether I should switch trams. He looked up suddenly in my direction. My tram began to move. I turned in my seat towards him, but all I could see was the nape of his neck. His head had bent forwards as if he'd instantly fallen asleep. Or died.

I was often sure my father was dead, but then he'd appear in some unexpected corner.

His hair doesn't thin. Gradually it is turning grey, but it seems as thick as it was twenty years ago. He's small, I never noticed it before. I would definitely tower above him in my high-heeled boots. He goes around and tells everyone I'm his daughter. "Your father's standing outside the door," say my colleagues. They're irritated. "Hey, he's been standing for nearly two hours in the cold." "He's here early! Are you going to eat together?" I can see him through the toilet window if I stand on the radiator and peer downwards. He's got a newspaper pinned under his arm. He looks at his watch. He turns from side to side, searching. He reads the headlines. He goes to the porter's lodge. I can't see him any more. I wash my hands thoroughly and leave the toilet. I get my coat, take the lift to the ground floor and wish the porter "Bon Appetit". I put on a disgruntled expression, which immediately falls away: My father has disappeared.

*

It started, half a year after my first communion, with suspected appendicitis, according to the GP. My mother went to the hospital early on New Year's Eve. Since my father hadn't come home, she left a message at his office as well as a note on the dining table, then she took us kids to the neighbours, her back buckled by pain and taking tiny tapping steps, which horrified us so much that we laughed. And finally she let the ambulance drive her away.

In the evening she phoned us at the neighbours and wished each of us a Happy New Year, and one after another we sobbed into the receiver and couldn't answer her.

Two tumours were removed along with her appendix. The doctors congratulated my mother: she'd acted quickly and correctly. On the 2nd of January, my father reappeared with a young woman, who would look after us for as long as my mother was in the hospital. "This is Rebecca." Then he was gone again.

I have often imagined that my father was dead. Sometimes I've given him the Last Rites. Sometimes I've spat on his frozen eyelids.

We have to be quiet. I'm eleven years old and no one must know anything. "We've moved house, end of story," my mother says is what we should say. We've moved to a rented apartment in another neighbourhood. Since my father is already known as a customer of the electricity company, a box has been brought to the cellar of the new apartment next to the electricity meter, into which we must insert coins in order to get electricity. Sometimes it suddenly goes dark and the washing machine stops. Then one of us looks for the torch, the other for change, and another runs down to the cellar and drops in the coins. It rattles loudly, when the coins fall. Actually we should only put in coins late at night, so as not to be seen. And yet the grey box hangs, fully visible, in the communal laundry-room. Everyone knows that it's only been there since we've moved in. "No one should be asking any questions," says my mother. "We don't owe anyone an explanation."

*

Just before I encounter my father and the unknown woman at the seaside promenade, they find another tumour in my mother's colon at her biannual check-up. "Tiny," says my mother, "it'll be out in a second, you'll see." She was in the hospital for two weeks. I thought it was wonderful. Meals-on-wheels came twice a day and delivered its menu, which we threw, still lukewarm, into a garbage bag. Otherwise we were left alone. I phoned my mother mornings and evenings at seven and informed her that everything was fine. I saw my father every day when he left the bathroom and got fresh clothes from the wardrobe. Sometimes he was there in the evening, bought us pizza and then let us watch whatever we wanted on television for as long as we wanted. I was sorry my mother was discharged from hospital, but when she was home again, she looked so awful that I cried. Then she cried too, and comforted me at the same time. But it didn't work.

*

I come home from school. My mother had asked me that morning to help her with the shopping. She dictated the list to me. "And yogurt. No, wait, no yogurt. But fruit, write down: Apples." Then she remembered it was Wednesday.

"Aren't you working in the café this afternoon?"

"No."

"Why not?"

"Because Storrer doesn't need me today."

"Have you messed up?"

"Leave me alone." She always thinks that one of us will take after our father, gambling away money, drinking on the sly or getting into fights. I can't be bothered to keep on reassuring her and trying to prove to her that my conscience is clear. Now I come home and she's not there. There's no note on the dining table. It worries me.

My father has had an epileptic fit. He has to stay overnight in the hospital so they can watch him; my mother went too, so overcome with worry she almost forgot about her children for the first time in her life. She phones and asks whether we're alright on our own. The next morning, after she's picked him up, she explains to us in a strange, celebratory tone that she's spoken to our father. Everything will be alright now. He'll go to rehab. My father nods. Then he changes into clean clothes and goes out.

I have often wished that my father were dead. But he lives on. I don't know where and I don't want to think about how, but he lives, turns up every few years and kicks against my life.

Once I was walking home at night after meeting up with a friend. It was spring, the cherry blossoms were flowering and, even in the dark, they made the entire street shimmer pink. I saw a couple swaying towards me as if in a time loop. The man's face shone pink; the woman's remained hidden. The woman sang a kind of lullaby in a deep, gurgling voice. The man stumbled, she held him up and stopped singing now and again in order to laugh loudly. She was very fat. I only saw that she was black when I was a few steps closer, and I saw she was old in the same moment that I recognised the man as my father. He'd already bypassed me. I'd never seen him that drunk before.

I follow them for a few steps, then I overtake them and

stand in their way. I look my father in the eye, search his gaze, but his eyes are swimming, he can't focus, his eyelids flutter. He doesn't recognise me. He looks fearful. Suddenly he puts his hands in front of his face. The black woman tries to pull him onwards, past me. She's talking at him in a language I've never heard before. I turn away. Behind me the woman sings on, and after some time I hear her laugh out loud again. The garden fence next to me has a broken slat. I break it off, go after them and beat him up. The woman laughs. And I do it to her too. Then it's quiet.

*

Since I turned seventeen, my father has been dead to me. That spring, just before Easter, my mother had to have another operation: it was already the third relapse in three and a half years but she had a chance of recovery. "There's a chance, absolutely," said the oncologist in conversation with us *relatives*. As I was preparing dinner, the phone rang. "I'm not here," my father shouted at me. He sat on the leather armchair in his dressing gown with a glass of brandy, made a dismissive hand gesture and hissed: "Idiots". I answered with my first and second name. A Mr Doubt apologised sincerely for disturbing us "in this difficult situation". He was very sorry, even if he weren't personally acquainted with my mother. "Why," I asked horrified, "what's wrong with my mother?" "Yes, um, yes, my deepest condolences. Could I quickly speak to your father please?"

"Are you from the hospital?"

"No, but I'm a business acquaintance of your father."

"He's not here."

"I find that hard to believe. Please go and check."

"He's not here!"

"Listen, I urgently advise him in his best interest to—"

I hung up.

My father didn't even want to know his name.

"You're telling people Mum's died?"

"Stupid girl. Just leave me alone, all of you!"

My father has fallen asleep in the leather armchair. He jerks in his sleep like the downstairs neighbor's sick bulldog that sleeps outside on the balcony in the afternoons. The brandy runs out of the glass in his limp hand onto the floor. His dressing gown falls open. I see his short, fat dick, standing out dark against the white terry cloth and I can barely manage, despite my disgust, to turn my gaze away.

The next day he left. He simply vanished, from one moment to the next, and was never seen again, not even at the hospital. No, once, he brought her a box of chocolates. It stood red and gleaming on her bedside table. She didn't want to talk about it, she was worked-up and confused. He didn't come when we interred her ashes. When I was still small and I informed him with horror that he would die someday, since my sister had just told me so, my father said to me: "You've got to learn to let go, of people too: you won't ever see them again." I often thought about that sentence, in the graveyard as well, and about how I answered:

"Not me."

"Yes, you too."

"And you, Dad?"

"Yes, me too. It's not so hard, you'll see."

*

My colleagues haven't warned me. I wish the porter 'Bon Appetit' and smile at his compliment about my new haircut. "For spring," I say and wave at him as I pass. Then I see him. He stands in my way. "Hello." His voice sounds softer than before. I want to keep on walking. He grabs my sleeve: "I just want to talk to you."

Moles

He sits on the edge of the bed in his underpants, fanning himself. His dark brown hands dance in front of his pale thin chest, which he so despises, hiding it under his shirt, away from the daylight and from strangers' eyes. He's closed the heavy acrylic curtains, wiping out the white sun-spots on the mattress, and switched on the bed-lamp. His gaze passes over the telephone on the bedside table. He falls back on the mattress and reaches for the book again.

'Like every evening, Bovet stood in the open doorway and looked out into the darkness. He breathed in deeply, closed his hands like a funnel over his mouth and hurled his revulsion into the surrounding loneliness: *Just stay away! Keep off!* He thought of Solange as he locked the door for the night, and smiled inwardly. The plump spinster had, in his memory, remained graceful and elfine, just as he'd imagined her as a little boy. *Arthur,* he heard Solange's voice and saw her cradle the huge pillow in her arms. *Off to bed!'*

He forces himself to read it slowly, word for word, restraining his eagerness; the words droning in his hot head. *Arthur! Keep away! Shoo!* He dozes off, dreaming of Solange and her huge pillow. She looks like his mother in the dream; she shakes the pillow and out come millions of freckles. She smiles enchantingly: *Here is your life's story,* she calls, blows a kiss at him and waves goodbye. He wakes up. The lamplight is blinding; his head rests heavily on the book. He turns to the phone. He picks up the receiver and waits for the dial tone; straightaway, he puts it down again, wonders whether he should call reception and have the maid come up with a bottle of water or coffee or both, before deciding against it.

He turns on the tap, bends and drinks. He holds his head under the water and hears a ringing sound. Does he hear ringing? He turns the tap off jerkily and listens. Water runs into his eyes. The phone stays mute.

Without thinking, he writes his initials in the front of the book with a ballpoint pen. Then he looks at the two letters and shakes his head. He found the book in the hotel corridor, on the maid's cleaning trolley. He heard her hoovering in the next room and, giving in to a sudden impulse, he pulled the book out of the trolley's rubbish compartment and disappeared with it into his room, wiping his hands quickly on a towel.

He leafs through the book and can't find the place where he'd fallen asleep. The book has been well-read. The rough, porous paper is stained and swollen; the spine criss-crossed with creases, and squished mosquitoes lie buried in-between the pages. His powerful dark fingers rummage through the book; his eyes fly over the lines.

He tries to remember. He stopped reading at the part with the fairy and the freckles. Where the old, lonely Arthur Bovet thinks of Solange – his father's woman – who told him as a child that moles on one's skin represent a life's story. Solange claimed that he who has many moles can expect an exciting, wild and rich life. She said a fairy came in the night and shook a huge pillowcase, scattering the freckles.

Now he remembers it exactly. He'd just read the part where, for Arthur, the fairy always looked like Solange. For him, little Arthur Bovet, it seemed like the story-teller and the character melted into one being. Until now. Yes, that's where he stopped reading.

He hears footsteps in the corridor. He puts on a shirt and opens the door. The chambermaid brings fresh towels. He blames her for interrupting his reading. *When else can I do it?* she says. *You haven't left the room once. You watched me make the bed and fluff up the pillows. You saw it.* He takes the towels from her and slams the door shut. *You never leave the room anyway,* calls the maid through the door.

He fetches the journeyman's cloth bindle from the wardrobe, in which he's carefully tidied away his gear – jacket, vest, bell-bottoms, collarless shirt, broad-rimmed hat, journeyman's cravat, handkerchief, shoes and woodturned walking stick. He spreads the cloth out on the mattress and packs up the bundle. Toiletries, underwear, shirts, tools. He attaches the tied-up wad to the yardstick and is satisfied.

Hey, you, I'm ready, he says to the telephone, spoiling for a fight. *Dear God, South Africa, do you hear me? Not Aarhus, Granada or Dubai, but Cape Town. I don't want to learn Spanish, Danish or Arabic, but English, because I can already speak it a little,* **do you hear me?** He glares at the phone.

He leafs through the book, looks through it and thinks, I already know all that: How the young man arrives at Bovet's out-of-the-way farm; how Bovet says, *the roof's leaking* when the boy enters the room; how the boy answers, *I'll repair your roof in exchange for bed and breakfast*; how the older man says, *if you like* and goes to bed; how he lies there, the old Bovet, for the rest of the story; he won't get up anymore; he'll undress, lie down and think about his own death; how he wants to think about it, but instead he'll think about his life again, which remains a mystery to him, arbitrary and lacking a central thread, even in hindsight.

I already know all that, he thinks, but he's not sure if he's read it or not.

He stands in the shower and rinses himself with cold water, the nipples of his hated chest hardening. They disgust him. He listens for the sound of ringing while in the shower, through the thundering stream of water. Still wet, he lies in his bed and counts the moles on his skin. By one hundred and seventeen he has the feeling they've multiplied overnight or, he thinks, the fairy has struck again in the unguarded dark. He who has many moles can expect an exciting, wild, rich life, he thinks, and glances at the phone.

He calls the reception and orders a coffee. Then he opens the book randomly and reads.

'The young man looked for a place to sleep and something to eat. He decided on a room next to the stables, in which stood a bed and a chair. A picture on the wall, small curtains, nothing else. He found an open carton of milk and a chunk of chopped mutton in the fridge. The boy poured himself a glass of milk and spat it out again immediately. The milk tasted of blood, of goat and stable. He decided to start repairing the leaking roof, even though he had no idea what to do and hadn't been taught.'

He pauses and sniggers contemptuously. *Layabout,* he hisses. He then follows the eager-to-please young man of the book as he hopelessly attempts to fix the roof. As a result of the character's failures, he forgets the telephone, forgets to talk to God, even forgets about the heat.

A knock. He raises his head. He places his forefinger as a bookmark between the pages, turns on his side and gets up as quietly as possible, book in hand, the finger still jammed in. He stands beside the bed and stares at the dark green carpet. Another knock. The door opens. *I'm naked,* he says without looking up. He hears the surprise in his voice. The door closes again. Silence. *Mr Roeder, your order.* The voice of the chambermaid. He hurries into the bathroom with the book in his hand, stands behind the door and calls, *Yes!* The maid enters. *Sorry*, she says, and *here you go.* He hears her put the tray on the bedside table. He sticks his head round the door. *I'm sorry,* he says hoarsely.

He hasn't touched the coffee. He stares at the tray, the cup and the milk jug for a while before reading on again. 'The young man sat for hours at the old man's bedside and watched him. *What do you really want? Why don't you carry on? You've got your whole life ahead of you,* argues Bovet from time to time. The boy continues to watch him.

'*You've been lucky here,* the boy says suddenly and points out a mole on Bovet's arm. He gently pulls the covers away from the older man. *Here, look. That was the beginning. You should have kept to the north-west, directly towards this big mole,* he drives his finger at the mole on his collarbone, *but possibly your compass was lacking. You journeyed south: a mistake that almost everyone makes in a crisis. Everyone always thinks their instinct says south, yet south is almost always wrong.* The old man drew the covers up. *Get out. Just get out and leave me in peace, at last, some peace. Leave me,* he shouted, bitterly regretting that he had, in a sentimental moment, told the boy of Solange, the fairy and the pillow.'

He dips his forefinger in the cold coffee and licks it off. *Yuck.* He skims the next twenty pages, because he's thinking about complaining to the maid about the cold coffee. Then he laughs at the idea, shakes it out of his head, and dives back into the story.

'Bovet lay on his stomach and let himself be washed. The boy wrung the sponge out, put it away and trailed his fingertip down the old man's back. The water drops hung on his wrinkled skin like little magnifying glasses. *Can you paint by numbers?* asked the boy. *You join them up, from number to number, and make a picture.* He laughed. *Only, the moles don't have any numbers, so it's not easy to find a path, here and there, to make a picture: a bird.*'

He reaches for the handset and dials the number of the reception. Not to complain, no, only to ask for the maid to come again. He hasn't thought of an excuse. *Read to me,* he thinks he could say. *Read my moles. I'd like to know what lies before me, what I can expect.* When he hears the concierge's voice, he puts the phone down.

A Tendency
towards Nothing

Nothingness is the material which holds, and does not hold, the things of this world in balance.

Alfred Döblin

Our lucky partnership existed for over a year. We'd lost everything for the first time and were just laughing about it when, as we were leaving the casino on the 13th of September, Frank asked me if he could drive me home. His offer went against the rules – I didn't need to remind him – and it annoyed me.

Why? I asked.

Because it's Autumn, because today is Saturday, because we've lost and because it's nice to break the rules. Right?

He winked at me.

It was probably my guilty conscience which discerned a forbidding undertone.

I don't know. I tried to sound like I didn't care.

He winked again. *Yes, yes.* And added, almost in a whisper: *Good that we're not gambling, your face speaks volumes!*

I ignored this.

Where's your car?

Here actually. He turned in a circle. *Is this for real? It's gone! But they're regular parking spaces! It must have just rolled away!*

Frank, don't take this the wrong way, but I'm calling a taxi.

Wait! Maybe it's over there?

Look, these shoes aren't made for walking.

It's over there, definitely!

*

Since May last year we've been going to the Casino on the 13th of every month.

We always went in with the same stake, played for exactly three hours and stopped, no matter where we stood. It was forbidden to exchange further money: we stuck to the original stake. At the end we added up the winnings – or, if we lost, what was left of the stake – and divided it in two. Every time. We played French roulette at the same table, but separately.

'We're a lucky team,' said Frank.

We didn't have any contact outside of the casino. We met in the evening at five to eleven at night. We went home alone just before two o'clock in the morning. We paid for the drinks in turns using chips. We agreed on the drink, usually beer; we only ordered if the other was drinking. *Another beer?* Meant: *I hope you're as thirsty as I am.*

Frank had beautiful, dark curls. Exactly like the cellist from the first concert of my life, who's unbridled passion made me, just turned twelve, make up my mind to marry him. He and his cello had clearly been suffering as a result of their unsatisfied desire, but no one apart from me seemed to notice their distress and I wanted to jump up and call out: *here, here I am*. I have never forgotten him. Or, at least, I've never forgotten his curls.

The first personal question I asked Frank was whether he knew Dvořák's cello concert.

Which one? he asked.

Is there more than one?

No idea! He didn't seem eager to stick to the subject.

I never wanted to marry Frank, by the way. But I loved his curls so much that I'd look forward to every 13th day of the month: I'd take a long time planning my outfit, get ready just before six, and then find that the evening dragged endlessly until the clock struck eleven.

This particular 13th of May began as a bright sunny Sunday morning, but I was worn out and I didn't want to see anything, neither the bright Spring morning nor the grey, spent faces which reminded me of my own. The tram had hardly left the station before it braked hard and, after a long screech, came to a stop on an open stretch of track. Blinking, I looked into the eyes of the man opposite me, whose dark-haired head had, during the emergency stop, come so close to mine that I could smell the cold cigarette smoke and stale aftershave. *What's going on?* he asked me.

I shrugged.

He tried to open the window, but it could only be opened by tilting it a little. *I can't see anything.*

What's there to see anyway?

Maybe someone's dumped an old sofa. He laughed at his own joke. *Or maybe something awful has just happened to the driver and he's got to think about it in peace for a while.*

Most of the passengers pushed their way to the windows,

but no-one talked much. Someone said: *They could at least make an announcement!*

Another said: *If they'd already known that the way's blocked, they should have let people know beforehand and not have let them get on!*

I leant back and looked out of the window. The trees' light green leaves danced easily in the sunlight. There was hardly any traffic on the roads. My eyes closed. *Dear passengers, our journey is delayed due to an incident involving a person on the track.* The connection crackled. I blinked. The man opposite looked at me. *An incident!*

I nodded and closed my eyes again. I could feel his look settling on me through my eye-lids. I felt naked. *What is it?*

Who would kill themselves on a morning like this?

I don't know. Please don't look at me like that.

I sighed, resigned.

Are you tired?

Yes.

I'm tired too. Why today? Why here?

I opened my eyes. And sighed even deeper. *Because,* I let my gaze wander freely, *because he spent last night in that casino over there and lost the shirt off his back.*

I see, said my counterpart. *As clear as day! Do you gamble?*

I had to laugh. *I've never been inside there my whole life.* I hesitated briefly: *Do you know Dvořák's cello concerto?*

We met at five to eleven at night in evening attire, well-rested, showered and perfumed.

Will they let you in without a tie?

He nodded. *The dress code merely requires a jacket.*

You know the place?

Yes, I was here once before.

We agreed on roulette; in other words, he suggested the *Classic* and I didn't have any objections, seeing as I'd never thought about what kind of games were played in a casino before. *Please let it be French,* he said. *American roulette hasn't got any style, you'll see.* He took my hand.

I really only came to gamble.

Me too, he answered.

I'll always remember that first night with particular fondness. I was bored. Frank explained the rules as we played and so he had to teach me one exception after another.

Good, Frank, now I know what could theoretically happen if I put down an inside bet and zero comes up. Whatever an inside bet is!

An inside bet is—

Just tell me what I have to do to play the game!

He grasped my hand holding the chip, pulled it a little way across the roulette table and let go suddenly, so that the chip landed hard on the roulette table:

Now put the chip there. Nothing more. Now you've got to wait. Thirty-three! Black! Look, you've won. That's how it works.

I liked that.

When Frank called *That's a wrap!* at exactly two o'clock, I was disappointed. *Already?* In my silk purse there were just as many chips as there were at the start. I hadn't lost or won any. By contrast Frank had almost doubled his stake. He gave me half. *That's how we'll always do it from now on,* he said.

And what's in it for you?

You'll see.

In the beginning it was difficult for me to see him go. Not that I yearned to be near him, but I felt I was inexplicably bound to him. As if he were my employer. I, his secretary. The woman without whose help he would never remember his full name, let alone his birthday. The woman who got by without asking any questions. The woman who set down his coffee, put down his documents, seated his visitors; who gave him a sign to remind him about an out-of-office appointment; who randomly, but thoroughly, brushed the dandruff from his collar; who handed him the umbrella or the ticket or the car keys. Or, if he went out in the evening with his wife, the theatre tickets, the wedding gift, the bunch of flowers.

Frank simply had the most beautiful curls that I, in my twenty-five years, had ever seen. Everything else was beside the point. Our relationship was in no way comparable to a boss and his secretary. You couldn't even have called it a relationship. Nothing connected us apart from some gambling rules, which we both followed. And yet, in the beginning, it was difficult for me to say goodbye at two in the morning, and more difficult still to turn around and leave. I looked back once and in the last moment managed to stop myself from asking, *Will you be okay?*

He was okay. How, I would never find out, nor with whom. Actually, the only thing I knew was that he worked in a bank. But I didn't know which one or what he did there, because it didn't interest me at all. I knew his star sign (Leo), his shoe size (forty-four, *unfortunately not represented on the Roulette wheel*), his favourite colour (black). Every time he placed a bet on Black, he said: *My favourite colour.* And every time I replied: *Black isn't a colour.* And he said: *The total, the queen of the colours!* Apart from that I knew he never ate in the evenings because it prevented him from sleeping; he never drank beer outside of the casino, and he found saunas unhygienic. How we came to that topic remains a mystery to me even now, because we didn't talk *'at the table'* – as he sometimes said as a joke – at least, we didn't talk about anything which didn't directly relate to the game. Still, even now, I hear him saying, clearly and contemptuously: *Saunas are unhygienic, doesn't matter which way you look at it.*

I thought about us of course. Just before and just after every 13th. But it didn't lead anywhere. It is what it is, I told myself: Nothing. From month to month, I got used to this lack of commitment, even though on every 13th I'd assume he wouldn't show up and was always pleasantly surprised when he did.

    I lost every time. In fact, it would always look good until just past midnight, my little purse bulging with chips, but come two o'clock I could easily hold the remaining few chips stacked in a neat roll in one hand. Frank, by contrast, won without exception, and continually increased his wins with each visit; despite the fact that, just before midnight, it never usually looked good for him and he'd regularly ask me whether he'd be allowed to go to the counter and exchange more money. *No,* I said then, quick and sharp, and he smiled, stayed in his seat, put everything on the third dozen and won; put everything on the last corner and won; put everything on zero and won. At the end, he split it with me, and he did it without showing the least emotion – no funny look, no comment or joke. When he handed over my half I accepted it just as emotionlessly, although the suggestion that he should go to the casino alone in the future and keep his winnings to himself lay fully-formed on my tongue. Afterwards I always had more money than I did before, and I got used to going to a fashion store at the end of the month to buy a dress or a blazer, a pair of boots or a scarf for the next 13th.

At our fourth meeting, on the 13th of August, I brought a present along for him. As a Leo, it would have been his birthday around that time, but he wouldn't have wanted to reveal any more detail than that. *It's your birthday on the 17th,* I guessed, but he simply shook his curly-haired head, took the square-shaped package from me, grinned cheekily and said: *Let me guess. It's a CD.*

I nodded. *Maybe you can guess which one?*

For the life of me, no, I'm no fortune-teller.

It was Dvořák's cello concert. He looked at the cover blankly.

For me?

Yes, for you.

So. Jacqueline? A woman playing the cello? Isn't it a man's instrument?

Yes, I think so too.

But you're giving me the woman, he read: *Du Pré.*

It's the most beautiful recording I could find. And she reminds me of a cellist who I heard once at a concert.

That's nice of you. Thank you. Frank let the CD glide into the side pocket of his jacket and blew a kiss at my cheek.

We never spoke again about cellos or birthdays. I kept mine a secret too and didn't give anything to Frank the following year, but, when we met again at the entrance on the 13th of August, I said: *It's your birthday sometime soon. I wish you all the best.*

Better wish me luck!

Agreed. I wish you good luck.

You too! Come on, let's start!

The more Frank won and I lost, the less often I got round to playing my own game. One rule went: We play at the same table, but separately. I found it increasingly difficult to stick to it. I kept on removing bets I'd already placed as soon as he put his on the opposite side. If I'd decided to bet even and he on the other hand bet odd, I could hardly resist the urge to copy him and chase after his luck, which would, I assumed, always reside on his side. *We should stick to the rules,* Frank said, with a low voice and a thin smile, and I answered, made stupid by cowardice: *Don't worry, I'm following my insistent inner voice.*

Frank's smile vanished and he looked at me earnestly: *I'm relieved to hear it.*

And I looked back just as severely and nodded.

One of the croupiers spoke to me. He said he couldn't suss it out. He'd noticed me a few times. And I'd noticed him too because, despite being advanced in years and despite his impressive routine of pushing the croupier's stick across the green felt, he had a way of showing an unabashed curiosity, which his colleagues, with their profession's disinterested gaze, completely lacked. But I didn't tell him that.

He was mulling over the question of at what intervals I came to the casino.

It's quite simple, I replied.

Every two weeks?

No.

Once a month!

Yes.

On a particular day?

Yes.

I thought so. But which?

You'll find out for sure.

Frank didn't like to see me talking to the croupiers. I was

already waiting for him to suggest we should add such a ban to our rules. First, he followed the brief conversation with a moody glare. I smiled at him amiably: *Shall we get another drink?*

He shook his head. *I'm here to play, not get plastered. And not to gossip either,* he added.

Why was he so afraid? That the croupiers would talk to me about him, reveal something? Did he come here often, without me? With other women? Or with huge stakes?

Just after one o'clock, Frank had a tremendous run. He bet on *Passe* five times in a row and won five times. He put the winnings on *Cheval* eight to eleven, and eight came up. He bet on the small series: twenty-three came up. He put the total winnings on Black – thirty-one came up, and his mood was radiant. *Now I'd like another drink,* he said.

When he came back with the glasses of beer, I asked him straight out: *Do you come here often?*

Once a month, you know that, he replied, surprised.

Not more?

Of course not, that would be against our rules.

I didn't know that.

Now you know. And remember it please, it applies to you too. We both laughed because the thought that I could sit at this table without Frank was completely absurd.

Three evenings later, it was the 16th of January and after the supposedly coldest day of the year came the coldest night, and I entered the casino alone for the first time. I had to wait a few minutes before there was a free seat at the roulette table, but then I played rashly and determinedly, as if I were following a set plan. I felt as if I'd been liberated. I knew what I had to do at every moment; sometimes I bet wrong, sometimes right, and since I enjoyed the wins more than the losses, I felt as though I were surfing on the crest of a wave. After just an hour I'd tripled my stake and I went home happy.

I repeated the visit every few nights. On the 31st of January, I lost my entire stake for the first time in just twenty minutes, so I went to the counter and exchanged the same amount of money again. After half an hour that was gone too. I went home and gave up on any further visits until the 13th of February.

You're playing very defensively today, said Frank.

You're right, I sighed, *I don't have a good feeling today.*

Why's that?

Well, if only I knew!

Frank looked at me calmly. Then he shook himself, and put a whole tower of chips on Black: *My favourite colour.* He waited for my objection. But I said nothing.

On the 13th of May, just after midnight, I asked Frank whether, to celebrate the day, he wouldn't like to drink a beer on the terrace.

What are we celebrating?

It's our anniversary.

Frank fell silent.

So I tried again: *One year!*

Oh! He sounded relieved. *Well alright, but just a quick beer, we're not here to drink after all.*

And not to gossip either, I added in my head.

From the terrace we could see the railway track under the reflected light of the lantern. *Imagine, on a night like this,* I said. *He plays, he loses, he breaks off and drinks a beer here on the terrace, the night is mild, the crickets chirp, the tracks gleam.*

Who's HE?

The man who committed suicide.

Frank emptied his glass in one long draft. *Shall we?* He held the door open for me. On this night, Frank hardly won anything.

*

On this particular September 13th, it took a solid forty-three minutes of searching before we finally found his car and he put the right key in the lock and cleared the passenger seat.

Thanks for helping me.

Helped? I just followed you around.

Do you want to drive?

I don't have a licence!

Doesn't matter!

I can't do it at all. Frank, just drive already.

He kept on looking in my direction while he drove.

Do your feet hurt a lot?

It's okay, now that I'm sitting.

Strange feeling, isn't it?

That we lost?

Frank hesitated. *Yes. Or no.* He looked at me constantly, searching for the right words, while I nervously looked at the road. *Don't you think we're weird?*

Is that the question now? Could you please concentrate on the road! Frank! Careful!

The car crashed violently into a barrier.

I got out. There lay a body, not moving, bent double on its side on the road, a man with a thick woolly hat and a tattered down jacket. His breath rattled, and as I bent over him, he started to babble: a nonsense song, *Itty-bitty,* I heard, and *Honolulu.*

Are you hurt? Wait. I'll phone an ambulance.

But the man sang babbling on without answering, interrupted only by his short, rattling coughs.

Frank sat behind the steering wheel, staring ahead into the darkness. *I left my mobile at home,* he said simply.

He stepped on the accelerator; the car jumped forward. I instinctively hit the roof with the palm of my hand so that Frank braked in surprise. *Frank we've got to get help!* I got into the car. He drove off.

Three nights, three days he spent in my bed. He hardly spoke. He wanted the TV on the whole time, although he skipped tirelessly through all the channels, and he showered so many times that his curls loosened and his hands became wrinkled. Still, he didn't want to talk. On the second day, Monday the 15th of September, I advised him to at least phone in sick. I handed him my phone and left him alone for a while. He didn't eat the sandwich I brought him. On the third night he ordered a pizza, which he didn't touch. *Otherwise I won't be able to sleep,* he said. But he didn't sleep anyway. I caught myself – while making the coffee – singing the song that the injured man had sung. The images flashed quickly in my mind's eye, but as soon as I got into bed and handed Frank the coffee, they'd disappeared. *How are you?* Frank remained silent. *Please say something.* He remained silent. He didn't even want to repeat the question, which he asked me before the accident. On Tuesday night, Frank got up and put his clothes on. *He's definitely dead,* he said, before he went.

On this night I decided to report Frank. As Wednesday morning dawned grey, my decision dissolved into nothing.

On the 13th of October I waited at the entrance for an hour and then went home again. I didn't lock the door. I took a book out of the bookcase at random, *The Immortal Man* by Alfred Döblin, and allowed my hands to open it randomly. Page one hundred and forty-four. *Things have a tendency to roll towards nothing*, it said. I shut it again.

Dizziness

I have a friend whose name I'm not allowed to reveal (a shame, because she's really a remarkable woman) and whose story I'm not allowed to tell (a shame, because as far as I know, it's really a remarkable story). Yet she doesn't want me to do either. But I want to. Or should I say, I wanted to? If she allowed me to. And if I could. Since she (the friend, who perhaps is more of an acquaintance with whom I'd like to become friends) has not told me the whole of it (the story, which I'd like to impart) in all its details. Within it, gaps, holes, blank spaces gape open. I enter them, so that I can't fall in. I start to make it up instead.

Today was a good day – not a bad one, at least – a day of small, but confident steps. Like every morning, I did my balance exercises along the trunk of the oak tree: five steps there, five steps back, without repeating the same mistake I'd been making over the last few weeks, where I'd wanted to get to the end in a few, quick steps. One foot after another: slow, tentative, yet determined, I moved towards the abyss at the end of the tree trunk. I was only concerned with a single question and a single answer: Where should I put my foot down next – here, yes, I'll put it down here.

The insistent question, which I could only shake off after

a long struggle, was: What did the caller mean yesterday with the comment that we'd had better days, hadn't we? Whose days did she mean by that – mine? No, it's not going downhill; it's going straight on, along the oak tree, there and back and here again, every morning at the same time in the same spot in the forest.

Autumn has come quickly, quickly and thoroughly. Not quite overnight though, no. It was Autumn yesterday already. More in-between the time it takes for you to look again. In between.

I saw him only after I'd heard him breathing – intermittently and, it seemed, mechanically – just three steps away from me, at the foot of the hollow tree, which the spring storms have half torn down, leaving it standing there as if demolished. He was cowering by the bare tree-trunk, his backside pressed against the wooden stump, exhaling loudly, his arms leaning on his thighs, his eyes squinting. The head sunk low; the mouth wide open. Not old yet, not young anymore. Scared to death, he said, of a human voice, who's talking to him. You're killing me, he said.

A cool, clear morning, the sunlight breaks through the dewy vapour hanging like spider webs between the boughs and branches, the bright, hard light makes spots dance across the forest floor, across needles and leaves, twigs and stalks. Only the hollow tree remains dull and untouched.

Memory deceives. Or perhaps not. The days blur into each other and I think of him again, he, who I apparently scared to death yesterday, and I see him standing, rain-soaked, on slippery foliage, breathing the moist, heavy air out, breathing it out, out, out. My memories dizzy into one another, mix with each other; dance like the spots of light; creep over the tree stumps, nimbly up and down again; roll this way, and that way; they blur. Splashing in pools of memory, a sticky mire, where there is no weather, no season, no time of day. My memory also needs balance exercises, but where can I find a suitable tree-trunk that quickly? I rush through the forest on the look-out for one.

Toadstool! Again and again my sweeping gaze leaps back here, there, everywhere, every place, where one gleams unreally red out of the mossy darkness, like morse code, I swivel and swivel my head, blinking: three short, three long, three short, Beebeebeepbooboobooobeebeebeep.

So far as my memory goes, there aren't any here, least of all such big ones, such gleaming red-hatted ones. I talked to him. I believe I asked him, is everything alright? And I repeated it, because he didn't stop breathing loudly. So that I had to raise my voice to repeat it. His eyes suddenly sprang open and he screamed as if he'd seen something monstrous. Me. Then he exhaled so he could scream once more, louder than before. Incomprehensible – how he had that much breath without even inhaling.

Dizziness snuck in through the back door of my life, like all misfortunes. I first noticed it when it had completely overpowered me; at the same time, I realised I was unarmed. I would have laughed if someone had warned me in advance or if they'd suggested some defensive measures. But they didn't. They. Who cares about my dizziness? Who would have urged me to be careful in any way? My children have moved out. I live alone, hidden away. I am a completely private person: they still exist today and it's easy to be one. You are registered and notified. You pay your taxes. And already you're immersed in the legality of it all. I don't feel the need to issue information about my life, my thoughts and deeds, whether orally or through writing. And least of all through a worldwide web or forums. I keep myself to myself.

You're killing me, he said, when he stopped screaming. There was no answer for that. I've never seen this man before, never. Not for forty-seven years. Never have our lives touched. I don't want anything to do with his death. Please go away, he says, but I stay.

Today, I've picked up the thread again from where it tore yesterday. By the hollow tree. Just before reaching the oak tree trunk, which serves as a bridge, and where I do my daily balance exercises. Five steps there, five steps back, at eight o'clock in the morning, for seventy-three days. For as long as I've known it, my oak tree lies diagonally on the ground. It looks like it simply lay down there, calmly and determinedly, with the approval of its environment.

Without any sense of balance, I'm afraid that dizziness will eat up my life – and me, in other words – and not throw me up again. Dizziness has already raged in me for a month in total. Thinking is not possible, nor is doing anything, even when lying down: even drinking or blowing your nose is unthinkable. Small, determined steps. One after the other and one before the other; on and along the fallen tree.

Don't do it, I said. What else should I do? he asked. I see myself thinking about it. The toadstools are glowing. How many would he have to eat in order to reach his goal? As far as I know, the human consumption of toadstools has never been systematically researched up to the point of death. After all, who would offer themselves as a tester? He would be the suitable test person. I thought. Had our acquaintance not been so short I would have suggested it. Perhaps then he would have laughed. And forgotten about the rope. I thought, and fell silent. *Please go.* I just shook my head.

I thought of my son – no idea why. My son is a teacher, a Maths teacher at a secondary school. He teaches the first years, and it makes him unhappy. There wasn't any point in me studying for that, he says. I remembered this sentence. This man in front of me, not young anymore, but not old yet, had a red nose. He clutched it in his fist. Crouched down again. The other hand played with the rope. He'd already made the knot and tightened the loop. He was ready. He was prepared. He'd chosen a tree. He didn't say which. He grew louder. Go already. After a long pause, I said: What was the point of studying for this? I'd never seen such a surprised expression before. I looked at the ground.

At closer inspection, the foot of the tree was bustling with hundreds of yellow ladybirds, grouping together for their hibernation, streaming past, climbing, crawling and rolling with each other and over each other. Watch your step, I said. He followed my gaze. Best not make a wrong step, probably better to stand still? He looked at me. There we stood, two unique giant toadstools, stock still and upright. Him over there, me over here. When I noticed this, I began to talk. My daughter, as soon as she was able to walk, I said, *it* must have been here, in the oak forest, I drew her attention to a ladybird. The first of her life. She observed him for a while, pointed at him with her forefinger – her face lit up – and with a very slow, deliberate movement, she squished him. (It's a strange feeling to stare at someone while talking and be stared at in return.) Actually, the ladybirds are too late, I continued. A good month too late. They should have been asleep long ago. Good night! What a ruckus!

He turned away and sighed without my being able to tell why. I went on talking. By the way, the beetle would have played dead had he known of the danger posed by my daughter's forefinger. But he crawled over her open hand and let himself be squished without resistance. My daughter is grown up now. She's studying medicine. And then he suddenly turned to me and laughed: Medicine! To my surprise, the word amused him and he repeated it a few times, laughing briefly each time he did.

So, I didn't kill him off, I just put him off. From his scheme. I forgot my balance exercises and went home. I gave him my number before I went. In the afternoon the police phoned me. They found him in the forest, hanged. The only thing he had on him was my number. I know what he's called now. Was called. The police revealed his name. I didn't know who he was yesterday, but now I miss him. Friedrich Probst. The name doesn't suit him at all. I've got to go out and get some fresh air before the dizziness forces me to the floor.

The Swing

The First Attempt

Her mother's exaggerated excitment was the first thing that struck Melanie as she stepped through the glass doors of Arrivals. Her mother was clearly finding it difficult to stand still: she was pacing up and down; her head looking in all directions; hands flapping.

Melanie glimpsed her mother only briefly before she was spotted. At the same moment Melanie decided to make a break for it, her mother turned her restless head in her direction. Her arm shot up and she waved it about furiously. What was wrong with her? Melanie felt her mother's excitement spread through her like the flames of an Australian bushfire; she felt as though she were momentarily ablaze, unable to fight the fire. She hurried over to her mother. When will this end, she asked herself, how much farther must I go, how much longer must I stay away? If only I could for once, just once, observe my mother with calm detachment! If only I could just state, simply, and without getting upset: my mother is overexcited. They hadn't seen each other for a year. And it was already too late. It was already too late for the emotional embrace of an easy, happy reunion. They were caught in each others' gaze. They stood opposite each other, their mouths open, panicked and mute, until the mother finally managed to gasp, *Lydia. Lydia is here,* and the daughter, not understanding, repeated: *Lydia?*

Your Aunt Lydia!

Where?

Melanie, what does this mean?

And that was where it all started: Melanie said *I don't know* and the first lie was uttered. A lie? Without telling her mother, Melanie had been in contact with her aunt for several months. They wrote to one another. And Melanie remembered having informed her aunt in the last letter of her homecoming: 'I will spend my birthday (at least it's a round number!) in the air. Goodbye, Sydney! I'll be travelling for twenty seven hours (stopping on the way in Singapore). Can you hear my deep sigh? It's speeding in your direction, once around the world, towards home.' Yes, Melanie wrote this a month ago, but she hadn't counted on the fact that her aunt would make the effort to look up the arrival times in order to surprise her at the airport. She looked around. *I can't see her. Are you sure it was Lydia?*

Definitely.

They drove home together in silence. Melanie waited in vain for her mother to ask her questions.

The air hostess woke me up yesterday somewhere over the Indian ocean and surprised me with a tiny birthday cake and wished me an unforgettable day. Secretly she hoped that her mother would congratulate her too. But instead she stared intently at the road and said nothing.

Perhaps you remember, I turned thirty yesterday. Alice? Are you listening?

Her mother gives a start. *Yes? Why are you calling me Alice?*

You wanted me to.

I've got used to Mama.

And I've got used to Alice.

Melanie, was Lydia at the airport because of you?

Absolutely not. The second lie. And yet, Melanie had intended to tell her mother about the exchange of letters with her aunt. That didn't seem possible anymore. She'd even dreamt she could bring about a reconciliation between the sisters. That too was probably unlikely.

You know what Lydia did.

It was an accident!

If I were to deceive a blind man by lying to him that the pedestrian light is green, and he gets run over, is that an accident too?

Alice, Mama – the comparison is ridiculous!

Oh no! The pond is safe, dead safe, there's a fence around it, don't worry, she said.

How long ago was it? Twenty five years?

Twenty six. And for twenty-six years nothing has changed the fact that Philipp is dead.

*

Melanie slept for almost a week. Before she left for Australia, she could sleep through entire days. There was always a good reason for it: she was either stressed out by coursework or by exams and needed to offset it, which is how she explained it to her mother, who wondered how she could sleep so much and yet study so hard. In fact, Melanie only learnt by cramming, but she graduated twice with the highest grades. When she wasn't studying, she slept. Sleep was her friend and foe at the same time. She threw herself at his warm breast and allowed herself to be calmed, comforted and lulled. Above all, sleep let her forget. To forget that she still didn't know what it felt like to have a life independent from her mother, in her own apartment, with her own thoughts, caught up in her own problems. At the same time, she cursed the power of sleep, since it was responsible for her inactivity. When she woke up in the early evening with a heavy head, it was sleep's fault that, yet again, she hadn't done anything: she still hadn't moved out in order to find an aim in life, whether it was in the form of a bridegroom, a child or a career. When they ate dinner together, Melanie said nothing while her mother talked at great length about her day at work in the staff room and classrooms: laughed about clumsy colleagues, denounced the stupidity of local politicians and their new money saving schemes, described the learning and attention deficiencies of her special needs students, and how she'd personally passed the day, what she'd thought, what had annoyed her, what she'd learnt. That was a very important point. No dinner was complete without Alice declaring, *Let that be a lesson to me*.

Melanie nodded, smiled, asked questions. And where an anecdote was necessary, she put on an expression of interest, or sympathy, or happiness. She made the appropriate sounds to go with it, like *uhuh* and *ah* or *hm*.

Since her return from Sydney, Melanie turned up at these dinners only very briefly and twice slept through them altogether. *The time difference, no wonder,* said Alice. *Your body's readjusting; it's only natural. Have a good long sleep!*

Yes, answered Melanie, then, *Thanks*. And she couldn't decide whether she should say *thanks Alice* or *thanks Mama*.

She turned on her side and threw herself into sleep again, dived in, dreamt.

Someone tapped her shoulder from behind. She turned

round, *Where is Philipp?* Asked a man, at which point Melanie ran away, chased by this man, and on the look-out for her little brother, right through Redfern, an area of the city where she lived. Out of breath, she shouted Philipp's name, but no one took any notice, apart from the man behind her; she heard, she felt, his erratic breath on her neck; she ran on, *Philipp!* She arrived at a multi-storey car park, she ran up the spiral drive as beeping cars drove down. A lorry, she pressed her back against the concrete wall and the pursuer grabbed her, his mouth searching for hers, while his hands loosened her belt and yanked down her jeans. Over his shoulder Melanie saw the pleasing looks in the shocked eyes of the drivers, but no one stopped. Then she closed her eyes.

She repeatedly dreamt of sexual encounters with strange men on public streets, some of which she thoroughly enjoyed. The dreams mostly took place in the area of Sydney where she used to live. They had no connection with reality. In the whole year she was there she was invited out to dinner exactly once, where she immediately fell for Jake, with his green eyes, but he never called after the first night. Three weeks later, her love had completely transformed into hate, and Jake was clever enough to keep his distance, seeing as Melanie spent almost everyday thinking of new and painful ways to get back at him.

A few months ago, Philipp appeared in a dream for the first time. She'd bought a six-pack of beer on the way home, drinking it all within an hour in front of the TV while sketching a portrait of Jake in her chequered notebook, before cutting it into tiny strips with her nail scissors, forming a little paper ball, and throwing it with accuracy at the TV screen – hitting the early evening soap actor (who reminded her of someone) squarely between the eyes, which wasn't easy because the drama cut quickly between scenes, the performer rarely stood at the centre of the screen, and it was rarer still for him to be static enough to make a good target. At some point she fell asleep on the sofa. A small boy took her by the hand and led her away. When Melanie asked what he was planning to do with her, who he was and what he was called, he looked up at her, smiling. *There!* He repeated again and again. It seemed to be the only thing he could say. Melanie let herself be pulled into a garden where apple trees were flowering and a swing swayed in the wind. *Philipp, come sit on my lap.* She bent down so she could pick him up, but grasped at air. He was gone.

After this dream, Melanie started sending letters to Lydia. Her first thought on waking was to phone Alice. She had the phone in her hand already when she had the second thought of writing to Aunt Lydia. 'I dreamt of Philip. Even though I was so young myself back then, I can remember him clearly, but they are always the same memories,' she wrote. And it was always the same three, no matter how hard she tried to remember: she hugged him violently, pressing him close until he fidgeted or coughed, laughed or cried. She pushed him in a woven doll's pram while going for walks, until the pram broke. She fed him daisies, which he resisted, but she was strict: *Swallow!* 'Dear Lydia, why am I really writing to you? After all these years? From down under, from the other side of the world? That's what I ask myself. You didn't appear in my dream, but a garden with apple trees and a swing did. Was there a swing, back then, in your garden? Probably not, you didn't have any children. There was your pond, of course, and for me now, in hindsight, your whole garden seems to consist only of this pond.' She thought for a long time. Suddenly, she knew who the actor, whose face she'd used earlier that evening as target practice, reminded her of: her unknown father, of whom there was only a single photograph, taken before she was born. *Claude, 7.7.1979* was written on the back of the picture. And Melanie wanted to write to him too. But with just Claude and Lyon to go on she wasn't able to find an address. She picked up the letter to Lydia again: 'If you want, let me know your news. I'd love to hear from you. PS: What happened to Fritz?'

Second Attempt

Fritz was different. Lydia said. She trusted him more than her husband, Walter. She cared more for him. She was more loving towards him. And vice-versa. And yet Fritz was a dog, a cocker spaniel. A real Blue Roan, which was important to Lydia. He wasn't covered in black and white spots or dirty, like some ignorant people thought he was, but a pure-bred Blue Roan spaniel *with certificates*. He was different in that he always wanted to do his own thing. Lydia only had to open the terrace door and Fritz did the rest. He created his own exercise programme, managed the required run-around himself, and returned home when he'd had enough. He lay down in his basket and waited. As soon as Lydia spotted him, he wagged his tail at her and got a tasty treat. Lydia didn't care about what he did in the garden for hours. In the evening she sat with him in front of the TV and filed her nails or plucked her eyebrows. Every few minutes she said *my beauty*. Fritz nuzzled up to her and made satisfied smacking noises.

Fritz was also different in the way he demonstrated affection. Unfortunately, his joyful dances would often be misunderstood. What would he have done without Lydia as his interpreter? When he stormed at visitors, barking and jumping up at them, Lydia translated it as: *Say hello to me!*

I'm Fritz! I love visitors! When he snapped at their ankles, it meant something like: *Great to see you again at last. I've missed you so much.* And when he nipped someone, Lydia said: *I love you so much I want to gobble you all up.* Actually, no one could claim that Fritz was badly behaved, because a word from Lydia and he would do as he was told: stop, shut up and back away. But many visitors waited in vain for this order from her.

Walter, Lydia's husband, hated Fritz. The dog entered Lydia's life two years before he did. He had the feeling that he was disturbing the two of them from the start. He tried to ignore it. But as soon as the initial passion wore off he asked Lydia for separate bedrooms, since Fritz would creep into their bed, lie diagonally across it and snore loudly. Lydia agreed immediately.

Of course, you should have your own space, she said. Walter felt betrayed, but nodded and bought himself a new bed. Lydia took this as proof of his lack of interest. She viewed the reason he gave as an excuse, since she could not believe that Fritz could disturb anyone, no matter what Fritz did. Years later Lydia confessed that, from this moment on, they'd effectively been divorced, which outraged Walter, who claimed that, in the subsequent twelve years they were married, right up to the end, he'd been ready to work on the quality of their relationship. Walter waited for years for Fritz to die, under the impression that his marriage to Lydia would then breathe freely again; a gust of fresh air, bringing with it a new lease of life. After the *accident*, Walter fleetingly hoped that Fritz would be put to sleep and that the domestic problems would then be solved quicker than expected, but he should have known Lydia would never have agreed to it. Because even the *accident* didn't change her love for Fritz.

Nothing at all. Alice could say what she wanted, it didn't matter. Of course Lydia was deeply shaken by Philipp's death. Of course she could empathise with Alice, especially after the possibility of Fritz's death was mentioned, a possibility which silenced Lydia and caused her to cry endlessly. She cried more about the idea of putting Fritz to sleep than she did about the drowned Philipp. Who could blame her for it? The idea of Philipp's death seemed to her so abstract, the idea of Fritz's execution, by contrast, was horribly real.

Lydia always assumed the holes in the garden were fox's dens. She didn't know anything about Fritz's passion for digging until she learnt her nephew had drowned in the pond. Fritz had dug a hole under the fence in order to reach the water and Philipp followed him. At this point, Lydia was on holiday with Walter at the Costa del Azahar, admiring the orange blossom. Alice looked after Fritz and the house, moving-in for ten days with her two children. Every day Lydia phoned to ask after Fritz. On that day, Alice was monosyllabic. But Lydia wanted, as ever, to know every detail. *Is Fritz making a good impression? Is he in a good mood? Is he sleeping well? Does he have a good appetite? Has he cried? Are you brushing him thoroughly? And don't forget to clean his ears, that's most important. If there's a problem, I'll give you the number of the hotel.*

I already have the number.

Don't hesitate to call, okay?

I have to check up on the kids, Lydia.

When Lydia phoned again the next day, she couldn't reach Alice for hours, despite countless attempts. Both women were beside themselves when they finally got through to each other. It was a short conversation. Alice could hardly speak, she brought out single words and then hung up. Lydia understood this much: Philipp was dead and Fritz should, Alice demanded, be killed. She and Walter immediately returned home.

Twenty-six years later she wrote a reply to her niece in Australia.

'Dear Melanie. I got your letter even though the address was wrong. I hope that you're well (I also hope your mother is well too, by the way.)' Then she quickly moved on to focus on her garden, in which there had in fact been a rotten apple tree – she only remembered it when she read Melanie's letter – which bloomed every two years, but didn't provide any fruit and at some point was cut down. However – Melanie had been right to assume – there had never been a swing. The question about what happened to Fritz pleased Lydia the most. But, due to embarrassment, she kept to herself the fact that, with his death, she'd lost the only living being who she felt didn't reject or deceive her. 'You asked after Fritz and I have to tell you that he died seventeen years ago. He was fourteen years old, which is a pretty good age for a cocker spaniel. It's a long time ago now! But I still cry even now, while I'm writing this. Fritz's end was also the end of my marriage with Walter, with whom your mother Alice – I don't know whether you know (and I don't know whether it's right to tell you) – had an on-and-off affair.'

Third Attempt

There had only been two men in Alice's life, and she hadn't loved either of them. *They haven't got anything to do with it,* Alice claimed, (just as they don't have anything to do with this story). She stopped seeing Claude, the Lyonnaise Biology student, with whom she'd just had Melanie, during her pregnancy with Philipp. She did inform him of the birth and, in a brief message, revealed the name, date and time, height and weight, but nothing more. – No actually, she did write another line underneath, which she forgot about later: '*Je suis très heureuse.*'

Alice and Claude had, for a few years, *consorted*, as Alice liked to call it, although they'd never shared a house or made any plans for the future. She met him during her term abroad at the University of Lyon. Shortly afterwards, she waited in vain for her monthly bleeding and, after she spent the night drinking so much rum that she lost consciousness, she decided against an abortion. At the same time she promised Claude not to bother him anymore, and she kept her promise. If he felt like visiting her, he would come in a rented car and stay for a few days, and there was even a phase after Melanie's birth when Claude came too often, looked too proudly at his daughter and put too much emphasis on the words *ma fille* for Alice's liking. It surprised them both that Alice fell pregnant again. Claude carefully asked whether perhaps there weren't other gentlemen who could come into question as the progenitor. Alice answered: *Pas un seul*. It was their last conversation. The only other sign of life from Claude which Alice received was in the form of a letter he sent seven years ago for his son Philipp to open on his twentieth birthday. In all these years, Alice hadn't managed to tell Claude of the death of the son they had together. She threw the letter in the bin. Just before she tied the rubbish bag and put it outside the door, she fished it out again and put it in the drawer of her bedside table. One sleepless night she opened it. After reading it, she felt vindicated: she'd been right not to get back into contact with Claude.

The desperate affair with her in-law, Walter, still embarrassed Alice years later. It ended just as abruptly as it started, the night after Philipp's funeral.

The two sisters had got into a bad fight: each of them trying to fix the blame on their opponent, one accusation led to another, one slap to the next, followed by screams, shoves, kicks. *I'll never let Fritz be put down*, screamed Lydia. *You're the only one who's responsible for your children!* Alice threw herself at her sister, knocking her to the floor, and sat on her, just like twenty years ago when the younger sister regularly beat up the elder. She broke her nose and slapped her, until Lydia couldn't defend herself anymore but simply screamed so loudly that Alice let go to shield her ears. Then Walter stepped in. He grabbed Alice, pulled her up and held her in both arms. *Put some sense into her*, shouted Lydia, who got into her Mini Cooper and drove off with a bleeding nose. Walter and Alice exchanged a quick look before their mouths crashed together and they started kissing, even though it looked as if they were biting each other. What brought Alice and Walter together was nothing more than hate for Fritz, the cocker spaniel. They both knew it, even though they never said it.

There would often be weeks, sometimes months, separating their secret meetings. And it was always Walter who phoned to notify her of a good opportunity. Alice swore after every meeting that there wouldn't be another. One day Walter greeted her with the words: *I told Lydia everything.*

Good, answered Alice, and with that it was over.

For the time being.

Many years later Walter phoned again. He was free, he said, Fritz was dead and his marriage over. Alice agreed to meet him. At first sight, they both knew there was no longer any foundation for a relationship, and yet they agreed to meet again regularly in the following weeks and months. They did not have the courage to admit to the lack of passion, until one day they both realised three months had passed without seeing each other and they hadn't once missed each other, not even a little.

*

For the entire year, Alice missed Melanie. Sometimes it was so bad she could hardly wake up and get ready in the mornings. The thought of standing in front of a classroom made her dizzy, even though she had twenty-five years of experience. She sometimes phoned in sick, which made her feel worse and led her to doubt whether she'd ever be able to get up again. How often had she accused Melanie of being as dependent as a primary school pupil? *Find your own place and make sure to get by without me,* she'd demanded of her daughter. When Melanie told her she wanted to go to Australia for a year in order to work for a marine engineering company, developing new compound materials, Alice was both excited and uncertain, because she hadn't believed Melanie could do it, because she suddenly didn't know whether she agreed to it, and because she didn't have a clue what compound materials were anyway.

When Melanie was small, Alice often slapped her, for which she always reproached herself afterwards. But there was something inside her which wanted to lash out, even if she couldn't admit it to herself for a second. It had always been like that, but since she found Philipp, only twenty months old, face down in the pond, and Melanie next to him calmly playing with a little stick, while the dripping wet spaniel waltzed around the lawn – since then she'd directed her desire to lash out against Melanie, whom she loved unconditonally. It only stopped when Melanie, almost grown up, said that next time Alice hit her, Melanie would return the favour, and she wouldn't hold back. After that, Alice's hand didn't slip up anymore. Now, whenever they argued, to make up for the loss of this liberating arm movement, she fell into a desparate panic and felt terribly faint for days.

In reality Melanie found her mother's panic far worse than the slaps she used to get. Now there was no threat, as there had been with the hitting, which could help against it. Melanie felt helpless against these attacks of maternal feeling, and they quickly took possession of her too, burrowing into her, whirling inside her, paralysing her. The moment Melanie arrived, it seemed to her like she'd never been away. She and Alice seamlessly carried on where they'd left off a year ago. As if they were afraid the foundations of their relationship would begin to crumble if they started to discuss what was new in their lives, rather than constantly draw on the past which both brought them closer together and nearly suffocated them. Sydney was long gone as a subject: that file was closed, cleared away in order to make room for what happened a long time ago and which formed the foundation of the deep and strained relationship between mother and daughter: Philipp's death.

The one thing which remained with Melanie of Australia, after a week sleeping in her old bed, was the recurring dream of the TV actor or her father, she couldn't tell the difference, and these dreams were tangible, about run-ins with naked bodies, with no trace of tenderness, but filled with hunger and thirst and greed.

However, Alice slept better than she ever had before. After asking Melanie many times what Lydia's appearance at the airport meant, and after Melanie assured her convincingly that she knew nothing and doubted that it really was Lydia at all, suggesting that Alice simply phone her sister and ask her herself if the incident continued to bother her, Alice finally felt relieved and happy.

Of course this suggestion was a trick of Melanie's. She knew how to make herself sound believable. Over the years she'd learnt how to lie well and convincingly. Because she was not allowed to say the truth. How she hated it! There was so much Alice had so pointlessly forbidden. The three supporting walls of this Forbidden List included Claude, Philipp and Lydia. Melanie was also not allowed to ask about Claude, her father, least of all to express the wish of meeting him. On the 7th of October, Philipp's birthday, and 29th April, his death day, she had to put on a dignified, serious face, and there was no way she was allowed to seem untroubled or go out with her friends. And she was, of course, not to make any contact with Lydia. More than that, she was obliged to vehemently reject any approaches made by Lydia.

But now this is exactly what Melanie did do: she arranged to meet with her aunt. When she wrote to her from Sydney, the possibility of meeting had not been up for discussion, but already, with the final letter and Melanie's homecoming, the possibility was made real. Melanie hurried to finish the letter with the words: 'Please don't write to me at first, because I don't know where I'll be living yet.' It was never in question that she'd move back in with Alice on her return – where else? – but she desperately wanted to avoid Alice finding a letter addressed to her in the post box and see Lydia's handwriting (after all these years!) and – well, what then? Struck dead? Melanie's fantasies about her mother had always been pessimistic. When Alice stayed out late or didn't contact her when expected at a particular time, Melanie would worry terribly and fear the worst.

It was a quiet dinner. Alice seemed depressed, and Melanie's thoughts always moved around the same questions. *Tell me something,* Alice requested of her. Melanie shook her head and made a decision. That same evening she phoned Lydia, who asked three times if she were really speaking to Melanie.

Shall we meet?

Gladly.

They arranged to meet on Melanie's suggestion in a small café which was advertised with the words: *An Oasis of Calm.* There, the two sisters would meet each other again. There, Melanie would take her mother at the agreed time. There, the two sisters (hopefully) would not become overdramatic, foul-mouthed or abusive. Neither of them would faint or die of outrage. Melanie was going to risk it.

How shall we recognise each other? Lydia asked on the phone.

We'll recognise each other, Melanie answered calmly and resolutely, smiling a little.

The next day it looked like rain. Melanie sat for hours in the kitchen and held an empty glass of juice in her hand. At noon it cleared up. She buttered two slices of bread, dressed, and picked her mother up outside the school. They sat next to each other on the bench and ate the sandwiches. *Thanks,* said Alice and held Melanie's hand.

Come with me, replied Melanie and led her mother through the side-streets of the city centre. Two o'clock on the dot they stood outside the little café. Through the glass, Melanie caught sight of a lady who was sitting very upright. Alice held Melanie's hand and breathed deeply. *See, it was her. At the airport. Lydia.*

Melanie nodded.

The lady looked up and waved at them. She did not seem in the least surprised.

I can't do it, said Alice and turned to go. Melanie pulled her towards the entrance. *I can't do it,* repeated Alice quietly, as they entered the café.

The Nylon Costume

Leon fled screaming into his parent's bedroom and under their bed. He'd recognised him immediately. He would have recognised him in any disguise, because his father snores, even when he's not sleeping; he snores when he breathes. Whether he's walking up the stairs, driving his car or eating, even when he's completely motionless in front of the TV screen in the evenings, he snores as soon as he takes a breath.

His mother was the only person who said anything about it. *Jan, you have to do something, it sounds awful.* But since she died, no one's said anything and he snores, day and night, and it gets louder as it gets darker outside. Now it's just after six o'clock and it's dark, since summer time ended last night, and Jan's snoring is already clearly audible. He himself can't hear it. The only thing he notices is that he's started to sweat in his nylon costume. He's dressed up as a dead man for Halloween, because Leon wanted it. *As a dead man?* Leon nodded. *It's Hallow-een,* Leon said. *Everyone has to go as a dead person.* His father doesn't know this custom. *In my time,* he explained, *we used to dress up in February, for the Fasching carnival, as a clown or a cowboy. No,* Leon wouldn't let the idea go. *A dead person.*

He searched an online-auction site for a cheap black nylon one-piece suit with a white skeleton drawn on it and ordered a large size. Although annoyed by the high auction commissioning costs, he was relieved that the difficult decision-making regarding his convincing appearance as a dead person was now over. *He has to look real,* Leon demanded. Real. Jan always saw her before him. And she always looked the same. He'd tried so often to take pictures of her, with and without a camera, where he'd blink and try and keep her in his mind's eye, but these pictures were all either blurred or lost. Only this one picture remained: pale and weak in the hospital bed before the breathing apparatus was disconnected. She looked like a stranger, changed completely from who she had been a moment before, and he realised that someone had stepped between them, separating them. *Katrin,* he murmured, *Katrin,* as if he had to convince himself it was her.

Leon saw her. His father was against it but the in-laws insisted. *It will be important for him later,* they said. *When he's old enough it will be easier for him to understand that she's not coming back.* His father was under the impression that Leon understood full well that his mother was gone for ever, even now. And he would have liked to avoid the meeting – if you could call it such – between the dead mother and her five year old son. Leon stared at her, ran to his father and hid his face between his knees. He was scared to touch her and he didn't want to kiss her either. *Can I have an ice cream?* He asked in the corridor as his father carried him towards the exit.

Jan hopes that his skeleton-costume will fool Leon. He's able to sustain this hope because he hears his own snoring very rarely, and then only for a brief moment. He hears it now and again when holding a phone to his ear, waiting for it to ring. Most of the time, though, he blames it on the person on the other end of the line. If not, he just forgets about it again.

Leon never complains, nor has anyone else since Katrin's death. The snoring hasn't made it yet onto Jan's list of things that need to be changed for the better, and so it leads an undisturbed shadow-like life at his side.

Jan is sweating. The thin nylon costume has transformed into a padded ski-jacket and his stage-fright does the rest. In his armpits and behind the knees, under the strap of his underpants and in his crotch, he can feel liquid collecting.

I'll get you, he swears, inaudibly of course. He won't let the skeleton speak. Firstly, he's never heard a dead person speak; secondly, he wants to remain incognito. Of course, Leon already hears the familiar snoring before the skeleton steps into the room. Still, with barely a look, he screams and flees as if it's the end of the world; he screws up his eyes, struggles and twitches like a suffocating fish. The thought that he might be exaggerating it runs through Jan's overheated head. *I have to go to a conference in Munich tomorrow,* he said in the early evening before putting Leon to bed. *Anne's making your dinner.* Anne, the single neighbour whose daughters are, it seems, about to get married or have children. In the morning, he wheeled his suitcase to the door and said goodbye as if he were going on a round-the-world tour. Now he looks down at his screaming son and doesn't know whether he should feel guilty or be happy that his performance in the nylon costume is so succesful.

Out of shock, Leon forgets to ask the skeleton for sweets, and Jan lets his bony arms dance until the bag in his hand rattles to the rhythm. A few days ago, Leon told his baffled father that if the dead man didn't have enough currency on him, sweet-shaped currency, then Leon would unfortunately have to kill him. In the meantime, his father had researched Halloween customs and found out his son was wrong to claim everyone dressed up as a dead person. But so be it: the rules of the game were decided by Leon. So, that means sweets from a dead man. And: *he has to look real.* What does Leon imagine a real dead person looks like? Like his dead mother lying in the hospital bed? It is four months ago now. Already, or only? How accurate are these memories? One question leads to the other, and before Jan realises, they're coming at him from all directions, like an un-extinguishable *batterie* of heavy bowling balls, in the hundreds, falling, rolling towards him, but they never arrive, moving and at the same time frozen in mid-motion; incomprehensible and unanswerable.

Sometimes he doubted whether Leon remembered his mother at all. When Jan talked about her, Leon would change the subject to a grocery shop, the puzzle from last night, or the drawing he'd just begun. He drew a lot, mostly footballs and football players, or both, sometimes cars and roads, sometimes a tree, a dog, a bird. These drawings didn't offer any insight into what the loss of his mother meant to him. Was Leon secretly mourning? While sleeping? Was he plagued by burdensome dreams? But then would he sleep so quietly and so deeply by his side, night after night? Had Leon changed? The recent scene in the nursery where he ran beaming into Jan's arms, and in the next moment – his face contorted with roaring cries – began beating Jan's temples and adam's apple alternatively with hard, long punches, impossible to tame... Hadn't Katrin warned him of this, long before he'd experienced it himself? Also, Leon's habit of silently turning away to concentrate on another activity when he was asked a question – was this new too? Katrin had always answered everything he wanted to know about his son. There are people who speak with their dead, but he's not one of them. He doesn't ask her questions anymore, only questions himself when he thinks of her – all those questions, which roll towards him in their hundreds and make him dizzy: only they remain. Some have beaks, which hammer against the outer membrane of his brain, as long and hard and just as un-tameable as the unleashed fists of his son.

And so the skeleton dances. It shimmies its arms, swings its bag and performs a lively dance-step with its feet – which it learnt once but never used – and when he finally finds the right rhythm and carefully starts to move towards the still-screaming Leon, the child ducks down and runs off. The dance act comes to an end. The skeleton is no less hot than he was before, rather the opposite. He stands still and listens. Leon runs into the bedroom where the screeching stops abruptly and his father hears him crawl under the marital bed. Then it's silent. He follows his son with heavy steps, stomping down the corridor as if he weighed several tons – a maverick, unconventional interpretation of his role – and stops in the open doorway of the bedroom.

Leon lies in the dark and tries not to breathe. His father stands in the doorway with his hand on the light switch, ready to press it at any moment. Still, it is silent. Only the snoring breath of the skeleton. On his tummy under the bed, Leon can't help but fidget with excitement, his legs grinding against the carpet.

The dead don't speak, said Jan to Leon four months ago as they ate ice cream in front of the hospital, which Leon had wanted after his last meeting with his mother. He said it because he couldn't think of anything else and because there was nothing to say. Yesterday, Leon said it to him. In a bright voice. Just like that, out of nowhere, at breakfast, while holding a spoon to his mouth. *The dead don't speak*. Then the spoonful of porridge disappeared into his mouth. Jan took it as a stage direction.

Now he becomes uncomfortably aware of the limitations of his role. He has to say something. Something like: *hey, you, what are you looking for down there? Could it be the nice, yummy sweeties, I wonder?* With that he'd swing the bag again. He must do it: He would do it. He falls onto his knees and feels around in the dark for his son, finds a leg, grabs it, pulls at it. Leon screams. Jan grabs him with the other hand and with a quick jerk pulls him out from under the bed. Leon, flailing, defends himself. Jan gets up, wipes his forehead, turns the light switch on, and switches it off, and it instantly goes light then dark again. Leon gasps out of fear. Jan switches it on a third time. The light is blinding. Leon holds his hands over his head. His whole body is shaking, his eyes are blinking rapidly, his lips wobble. His father wants nothing more than to apologise. He feels helpless. He fails to remember. How was it before, last year at Halloween, Katrin, what did we do then? No, he resists this question. The dead don't speak.

He pushes his hands gently under the little, shivering body and lifts him up. In his arms, the shivering grows stronger, becomes a twitching, then a shaking which takes hold of all his limbs. He puts him on the bed and embraces Leon tightly. And then he does speak. *It's just me,* he says. *Leon, it's just me.* But Leon doesn't calm down.

The father takes off his skeleton-mask and starts to kiss the little quivering face, faster and faster, his lips gliding over his cheeks, temples, his nose and forehead, while his arms hold Leon and press him, tighter and tighter, until the father thinks he's the one being held.

He knows it's not right, but.... He sighs when he thinks about how it's worked out. For four months Leon has been sleeping with him in the double bed. The two lie next to each other. Leon gradually calming down under his father's caresses. Now he's hardly shaking anymore. Jan pulls back his hand, which was moving along the entire body of the five year old, and nudges him lightly: *do you want to go to sleep?* Leon wordlessly nuzzles his father. He continues to caress him. He knows it's not right, but he can feel Leon relaxing.

Jan lies awake and snores; Leon sleeps. He didn't ask how Munich was, nor did he ask, as he usually does, if his father had brought anything back with him.

Jan lies awake. He's thinking of all the festivals which take place during this dark time of year. St Martin, St Nicholas, St Sylvester and all the rest of them, these gentlemen. Not to forget the baby Jesus. And just after Christmas, it will be Leon's birthday: his sixth. Today's Halloween, that was just the beginning. There Leon suddenly started up: *Hand over the sweets or you're dead.* His voice sounded completely awake. *Dead,* he repeated. *Dead.* He finally accepted the bag, had a quick look inside and lay back down. *And? Will you let me live?* But Leon was already asleep.

Jan feels dizzy. He searches for an image. The image of her, the last one, the image that lies before the image he always sees. He searches for the image, just before death. But he sees only the one. The one where he hardly recognises her.

The blanket has come off. He draws it up and turns to Leon. He sleeps, silently, motionlessly. His chest-cage doesn't rise. His cheeks shine waxen in the light from the bedside lamp. He pinches him: Leon flinches softly.

Andante con moto

The second movement of Mendelssohn's Organ Sonata in C-Minor, which accompanied the small group on entering the church this Saturday morning, continued to reverberate in everyone's ears. Those with good hearing could still make out the bells from the start of the ceremony, which had rung while they all took their place, shuffling and coughing, on the dark wooden benches, wearing their Sunday best and freezing, because Sunday best is never the warmest outfit and they'd all removed their winter coats. They grouped together in a half-circle around the baptismal font: a hip-high marble vat at the centre of a small chapel in the side-nave, over which a well-fed angel hovered, merrily offering up a tiny golden ladle, which the pastor would soon take from him to perform Maxim's christening. Ines, his godmother, suddenly realised that Maxim and the angel looked alike, so exactly alike that she wanted to burst out laughing. She looked over at Sonja, Maxim's mother, who was clearly in no mood for laughing; bent over, pale and wretched, as if she were struggling with a powerful nausea. Ines couldn't know that Sonja was in the middle of the worst hangover of her life. She would never have guessed, because Sonja hadn't drunk alcohol for years. Until the day before.

To the right of Sonja sat her solemn-looking in-laws; on her left was the little Maxim, a thin thread of snot hanging from his left nostril. Ines focused on the thread, trying to banish it with her stare so that it might defy gravity and not drip onto the ironed christening gown. Maxim seemed to be wondering how he'd got there, in the middle of this circle of people. He looked around the circle with his mouth open, kneading the hem of the white blouse with his plump little hands. Ines looked around and caught sight of Maxim's father, Chris, standing next to a pillar behind the rows of pews. He avoided her gaze and stared first at the floor and then up towards the gallery in the direction of the organ, where the sexton was in a whispered conversation with the organist. Ines knew that Chris didn't even believe that this cold February would ever come to an end, let alone promises of healing and redemption. She only turned to face the front when Marc, her husband, nudged her, looking at her questioningly. She let him know she was alright with a smile, blowing a kiss at her daughter sitting on his lap, who didn't return it because her eyes were on the verge of closing; she fell asleep.

The pastor, who'd already greeted them with the explanation: 'The order of baptism is founded on Jesus' own words to his community', went on to add in a booming voice, imitating the Resurrected Christ: 'All power is given unto me in heaven and in earth!' At this moment, something fell on the floor and everyone turned around, shocked by the huge echo in the church. Everyone apart from Ines' daughter Lilith, who continued to sleep soundly on her father's lap. Magdalena felt fourteen eyes on her and blushed. She hadn't been invited. She was only there as a friend and weekend visitor of Ines and Marc. With her cheeks burning, she picked the camera up from the floor. She'd planned on recording the whole ceremony so that she could justify her presence in some way. She turned to face the pastor, who immediately composed himself with a quick straightening of his back, before repeating the section of his text so as to be sure that the words of the Lord could once again be eternalised on camera: 'All the power has been given unto me in heaven and in earth! So go forth and make disciples of all the nations, baptising them in the name of the father, and of the son and of the holy spirit!'

Thus ended the familiar summons of St Matthew's gospel; but here was also the beginning of something. The story of the Christian, Maxim. Where would the story lead, and how far would it go? Ines asked herself this question while waiting for her cue. She thought of herself as a fraud, even though she'd produced the required eligibility certificate from her Church that entitled her to act as godmother and confirmed her as part of the Christian community. She hadn't been a part of this congregation for a long time, and no one knew that better than herself, who'd once suffered from her childhood loss of piety. But she'd never found the opportunity or the determination to officially leave. When she filed away her salary slips, month after month, she'd be annoyed by the Church tax deducted from her income, and then, straightaway, she'd be annoyed by her own pettiness, since the Church tax only formed a small tranquil gulf in a vast sea of taxes, contributions and levies, nothing more. 'Your wish to have your child baptised is an expression of your belief that the Christian faith will be the path your child may follow for the rest of his life,' preached the pastor in the rehearsal christening last week, which the parents and godparents of the child 'were expected to attend'. Of course Chris refused to take part with the excuse that he was guaranteed to do everything wrong and would only hinder Maxim's christian path. So Sonja came on her own, thankful that at least Ines stood by her. The pastor was particularly insistent with her: 'We do not know each other yet,' he whispered to Ines. 'I haven't had the pleasure of Mrs Bergner's acquaintance for very long.' He was alluding to Sonja's own baptism, which only took place a week ago, rushed and forced, done in order to fulfil the terms of Maxim's christening. She was accepted into the community at Sunday service, and, in the absence of a godparent, the sexton stood in as a replacement: Mr Seifert, who was always blinking and never smiled. The Pastor, therefore, was especially interested in Ines as the future godmother, and continued to whisper to her in a strangely intimate tone: 'The godparent accompanies and leads the child on his Christian journey. It is clear, therefore, that you yourself must be on the same path!' Ines nodded, what else could she have done? And so she sat there now. At any moment she'd have to get up and step towards the font with Maxim, lift him up and answer the Pastor's question: 'Yes, with God's help.'

*

The night before the christening, Ines' pressure cooker exploded. She couldn't explain why. Marc later claimed she hadn't closed the lid properly, that she'd 'impatiently messed around with it until it jammed' like she usually did. Either that or the ventilation was defective; actually, this seemed to him the most probable cause, since it had been 'totally dirty and sticky'. Ines didn't know and didn't want to know. But what she did know for definite was that her life was completely ruined, just as useless, as unsightly and tragic as red cabbage on a kitchen ceiling. The longer she stared up at what was left from the cabbage's ascent to heaven, the more clearly she saw her life hanging there in dark red tatters, until she finally gave into the pressure from above and sank to the floor.

Strange, she'd never had an episode like that before. She'd tried to prevent it; day after day, she'd worked hard to find meaning in her everyday activities. It was easier to do that as an artist rather than a teacher, which she'd now unfortunately become. As a full-time job, time-wise, being a teacher was prioritised over being an artist, but she swore to herself that this wouldn't hinder her creative output. Other people had those kinds of crises, sure, because they believed for years and tens of years that it was enough to be financially and domestically secure in order to be happy and fulfilled, fulfilled with meaning. Other people had those kinds of crises, but surely not Ines, *the buxom*, as she called herself in some photo-collages; Ines, who could explode with laughter, but also with love, pride, happiness and gratitude. Ines, the forever wonderful, as her husband described her, because he didn't like the *buxom* at all and wanted to make a better suggestion, which was then rejected. 'No, *buxom* stays,' announced Ines after thinking it over for hours in her room, which used to be the pantry until Ines cleared out anything edible and put a chair inside. Since then, she'd been using this chair in order to think. That's what she was going to do now as soon as she found the strength to turn her gaze away from the ceiling and get up from the floor. She took three steps to the pantry door, opened it with a quick pull, threw herself on the chair and pulled the door shut just as quickly. She took her time to switch the light on. She closed her eyes, as if the darkness of the pantry was too bright for what she'd got planned, and tried hard to remember. She tried to remember the feelings she had towards life before the pressure cooker exploded. But nothing stirred. The light didn't change anything either; so she switched it on after a while. She continued to feel her way through the darkness of forgetfulness. It was just gone: not her past life, but its soundtrack.

*

The night before the christening, Sonja got drunk at her in-law's, despite intending it to be a short visit. She'd wanted to talk through the catering plans one last time – which would, for reasons of space, be taking place at her in-law's rather than the church – making sure they'd bought everything and had got everything ready. Sonja couldn't help it; she needed these numerous methods of control; it didn't matter if it was packing a suitcase, making a shopping list, the monthly bills or planned festivities like this one. Even the guest list, which really was very straightforward, had been checked ten times before she sent off the invitations to her in-laws and her bridesmaid Ines and family. Now she could again convince herself that all her checks were necessary, because her father in-law hadn't bought any meat, despite having insisted he would complete this task. 'Even better.' Grinning, he turned to face his son as Sonja pointed out his mistake in a quivering voice. 'Chris can come with me on the hunt.' Chris didn't say anything as usual, put on his jacket and trotted after his father. Left behind were a panicking Sonja, a placating mother in-law and an infant. 'I'm this close to losing it completely,' threatened Sonja. 'Maxim has to go to bed, my husband just disappears, and all your mollifying's getting on my nerves because nothing's ready for tomorrow!' 'Now there, there, my dear,' the mother in-law replied. 'We'll put the little one in the spare bed and we'll make ourselves comfortable.'

'Chris and Hugo will be back from the butcher's soon anyway so I'd rather wait to go home and put Maxim in his own bed!' But the two men didn't come back that soon, the mother in-law continued to insist and – Sonja couldn't believe her eyes – Maxim fell asleep straightaway in the unfamiliar bed. 'It never usually works,' she said and collapsed into one of the huge flower-patterned upholstered armchairs. She'd hardly sat down when the tears began to fall.

Horrified at first, she refused her mother in-law's Jägermeister out of habit. But then she remembered she'd weaned the baby a week ago. Up until recently breastfeeding had earned her a lot of head-shaking, even though she never did it in public, but there were certain other young mothers – Ines, for instance – who knew about it and who found it absurd and disgusting, because Maxim was almost two years old. Now he was weaned, after such a long time, she could celebrate the step with a glass of something. In any case, alcohol was good for drowning sorrows – at least the first glass was, then it tips over to the other side again, but she'd never drink more than one glass of Jägermeister anyway; she didn't like the taste, and there was nothing else in the house.

*

The night before the christening, just before ten, Magdalena arrived at the airport. She'd spent the last few days in almost spring-like temperatures in the south of the German-speaking world, where she'd often had headaches and was therefore glad when the captain, in his usual announcement before the descent, spoke of minus-temperatures in his weather report. Here in the North she would clear her head, take long walks in the icy air, spend a nice, relaxing weekend at Ines and Marc's, listen to stories from everyday life and worries unknown to her, and even attend a christening. She smiled at the thought, because she loved to do things which she didn't usually do, just as she loved foreign cuisine and exotic clothing.

She switched her mobile on and found a message from Ines: *Can't pick you up, little accident in the kitchen. I'll pay for your taxi.* And there it was again: the headache. Magdalena frowned and pulled her little suitcase towards the taxi stand where she was unlucky enough to get the only taxi driver in the city who was both a fan of folk music and hard of hearing. Although he understood the address surprisingly quickly. But no word after that. 'Could you turn the music down a little, please?' Nothing. 'Hello! The music is too loud!' Nothing. 'Please, I've got a throbbing headache. Switch it off!' Again, nothing.

As she walked up the endless steps to Ines and Marc's apartment, alternating light-flashes and black spots appeared before her eyes. Marc opened the door, 'Hey!' he cried. 'There you are!' He embraced Magdalena, she felt the wet cloth he had in his hand against her back. 'I've just got to remove some stains in the kitchen. Come in, take your coat off, make yourself at home.' Magdalena sat at the dining table and watched Marc cleaning. He stood on a ladder and washed the ceiling with wide flowing movements. 'Where is Ines?' Marc pointed at the pantry. 'Ah,' Madgdalena nodded and asked after a while. 'Do you think it'll take much longer?' Marc smiled. 'No, she'll come out soon for sure.'

Magdalena admired Marc. Admired his steadfastness. Her own husband was different in pretty much every way. Unfortunately? She thought about it. No, she loved Andi, despite everything, and in fact she'd never thought about exchanging him for anyone else. 'What happened?' asked Magdalena, looking up at the ceiling. 'Not worth talking about,' said Marc. 'Tell me, how are things with you?' My goodness, thought Magdalena, how Marc protects his wife, even with this kind of trifle. And Andi?

He says, 'I can't cope,' when I tell him I have cancer! Oh come on, she admonished herself, that's all over and forgotten. It was two years ago, and she didn't speak about it anymore: Marc and Ines had always accepted that and that was why it was so liberating to visit them. That whole chapter of illness was history, closed. She told herself this once more, as she replied: 'He's great, really, he has a lot of work on, but having lots of fun too. Do you happen to have any painkillers?'

*

Chris and his father came back late at night. They could hardly walk and had enjoyed, as they themselves expressed with difficulty, 'a boy's night out'. The father in-law was buoyant: 'We killed something too,' he boasted. 'Pre-skinned and diced, piggish in nature. Here, I'll put it here in the fridge. Hey, Gitte, now tell me you aren't impressed by that!' And his wife received a smacker of a kiss in the middle of her face. Chris looked moody and brooding. Sonja had, during the men's hunting trip, drunk five glasses of Jägermeister – it could have been six, although from the very first sip she'd felt the alcohol shooting into her blood, flickering in her brain.

She couldn't remember a single word of the conversation with her mother in-law, even though she knew they'd been talking non-stop and – no, it can't be, she'd forgotten that too – they'd cried together. 'Hello dear,' she said merrily. Chris stared at her in shock. 'I think we have to stay the night,' she continued and laughed so much that Chris couldn't understand anything anymore. His drunk wife unsettled him; she, on the other hand, didn't recognise any change in her husband and felt unexpectedly close to him as she collapsed next to him on the in-laws' spare bed, feeling twice as heavy than usual and without having even brushed her teeth – with what anyway?

*

It remained cold in the church, despite the pastor's heart-warming words. Ines actually wondered why she couldn't see any clouds of breath. He spoke of faith, of love and the hope that they'd become brothers and sisters: basically siamese triplets, a 'wonderful little gang', wherever one of them was, the other two gang-members would be there too. The pastor looked around the circle but, apart from the mother-in-law, no one else was smiling about his witty comparison, so he introduced a song that 'I'm sure you all know and hold dear. Please find the lyrics in the pamphlet.' He sang the first stanza to the tune of 'Thank You for this Beautiful Morning' alone, acapella, and with gusto:

Faith, that is the power of good,
Faith does evil withstand.
Faith gives us the strength to live,
Leads us hand in hand.

Magdalena was the only one to stand up and step forward, so she could get a better shot of the pastor. Out of the corner of Ines' eye, it looked as though the camera was moving nearer and nearer to his gullet as if to vanish down it, and again she felt the urge to laugh flickering upwards from her diaphragm, and she came close to letting herself go. She looked in vain at her lap, then in Chris' direction, whose moody face was often effective in putting the brakes on any fun; in fact, her urge to laugh disappeared as soon as she looked at his expression, because Chris was viewing what was happening with a look of deep despair, the only thing missing was for him to bury his face in his hands. 'And now everyone together!' ordered the pastor, and the small congregation bowed low over their song sheets and bravely sang together:

Hope is what every person needs,
Hope which God gives to all,
Hope he holds ready for anyone,
Who follows love's call.

Everyone sang along apart from Magdalena, who continued to film; Chris, who leant his despairing head against the pillar; and the two children, the over-awed Maxim and the sleeping Lilith. The little choir received strong support from the gallery: the organist and Mr Seifert, the sexton, both of whom were clearly not singing the song for the first time, despite the unusual lyrics. Ines, peering over the top of her pamphlet, observed everyone: Sonja still didn't look any better and struggled, with an ashen face and dulled voice, to synchronise the tune with the words; Marc, relaxed, with a contented expression, was even able to sing and gently caress Lilith with his big hands at the same time; and the in-laws demonstrated how to uphold a solemn countenance. But, after the third stanza, after:

Love leads you to every summit,
Love brings you through every dale.
Love, which today God gives you,
Will carry you and never fail!

Ines wanted nothing more than to spit it out, short and quick. She remembered the pastor's words, 'The Godparent accompanies and leads the child on his Christian way.' 'Accompany' and 'Lead' rang clear and echoed in her head. Only those who know the way can lead, she thought with a bitter taste in her mouth. But she didn't know the way, neither the ins nor outs, of any subject area, not one; neither a geographical area nor an area of knowledge. She felt least at home in the rugged area of her faith, which she'd travelled through once in early childhood, but which, perhaps, she could never recognise again. How should she find her way! Like a child at the helm! They want her to be a compass, as if she has the right to be one! As if parents, teachers, godparents have any right to teach children anything! As if they possess something valuable which others desperately need! It begins already with the surface, with appearance, the cursed physiognomy. Who is beautiful, healthy, functional enough to procreate? Who, in addition, has a suitable partner at their disposal? Ines looked at Lilith, then at Maxim. Surely it was a crime to reproduce. Lilith had inherited all the outwardly parental defects. Why were children guaranteed to get all the terrible flaws from both their parents? It was impossible to imagine what that might mean for Lilith (after all, at her tender age it was still far from clear and forseeable!)

Or for poor Maxim! His list would have to remain incomplete as Ines didn't know about all the possible shortcomings, but it went: sweaty feet and itchy skin, thin hair and brittle nails, flat and splayed feet, bad breath and migraines, dandruff and warts, varicose veins and sallow skin, bloated stomach and snotty nose. Added to that the tendency towards obesity, a weak back, a degenerating ligament in the knee, as well as thin lips, wide nose, fleshy ears, and a short neck. Bravo!

And now, on top of all that, as if he hadn't already been lumped with enough, he was being christened.

Sonja and Chris struck a decision only recently. That's wrong. Sonja struck it, struck it down, crashing, like an old, heavy, rotten tree. Noisily going against Chris' usual quiet, passive resistance. He was the type to chain himself to rail-tracks or even old trees, but that didn't help him this time. The idea of gathering together around the font came up around half a year ago, as a joke, it has to be said. Ines & Marc and Sonja & Chris had gone together with the kids for a day at the seaside.

In separate cars, of course, although they could all have sat comfortably in Marc's old mini-bus, but Sonja insisted on driving her own car so that they wouldn't be dependent on each other in case of an emergency. 'An emergency,' said Ines. 'What do you think will happen?' 'Something could happen to Maxim.' Ines couldn't think of anything that could happen to Maxim, apart from drowning, and in that case having your own car wouldn't help, but she thought it better not to say that out loud.

It was a hot day in August, and a Saturday. They reached the beach at St Peter's when the tide was out; the sea gleamed far away and looked as flat as a puddle, and in front of it waterways glimmered, meandering through the mud-flats. As soon as they got out of the car, the wind beat them hard around the ears, so loud, that they had to turn to each other and shout in order to make themselves understood. Without realising how strong the sun was, already beating down on them, they stomped, bare-footed, towards the shore. The men carried the children and the cool-boxes; the women blankets, clothing and nappies. They didn't have a windbreaker with them, so, once they'd spread out their blanket in a spot everyone agreed on, two people had to sit on it at all times to stop them from being blown away. The women sat down and the men and children raced into the cold water, as soon as they'd put on their wetsuits. Marc was clearly in his element, and it revealed a new, almost boisterous side of Chris. It stayed that way, with two short breaks when the men and kids emptied the cool boxes at a surprising speed. Sonja and Ines had a lot of time to talk, shuffling close together so as not to have to shout at each other. In this unfamiliar proximity the following conversation unwound:

'Chris is drinking more and more,' began Sonja, as she dug her toes into the sand, so deep they stuck in the ooze. Ines thought about it. 'More of it or more frequently?' she wanted to know. 'Constantly actually, and in crazy amounts. He disappears for days. I always find him at some point with the tramps in the park.' 'With the tramps?' 'Yes, he just sits with them. "May I introduce," he says, "the mother of my child, my best friend: Sonja. And here, Sonja, is Manni, Kricken and Födo. Shake their hands. And, how's things? How's life? How's it all going?" "What are you doing here?" He shrugs. "Forgetting." "Don't you want to come home?" "Nah." "Chris, please." "Later, sweetheart." But he says *sweetheart* in a way which makes it sound sarcastic, exaggerating the 's' sounds, like *sssssweetheart*. Despite wearing sunglasses, Sonja shields her eyes with her hand. She continues slowly: 'But what really worries me is that he hasn't gone to therapy or taken any tablets for two weeks.'

'Can't you mix it up in his food without his noticing?'

'He's run out and he can't face going to the doctor for a new prescription.'

'Can't you…'

'Can't you? I just can't hear it anymore! I've been doing this for years! I get his prescription, remind him about his therapy appointments and when he should take his pills, but everything keeps getting worse!'

'I understand.'

'No, Ines, I don't think you understand. It used to work before, when I was looking after him day and night. But since Maxim's come into the world, I just can't afford to do that anymore. Plus Maxim is a child who needs an unbelievable amount of attention.'

Ines thought: *You'd love that to be true, Sonja,* and said:

'Maxim seems like a completely normal kid to me.'

'No, he takes after his father.'

Ines fell silent. After a while Sonja grimly continued: 'He's totally fixed on me and loses all composure as soon as I'm gone or if something irritates him. He just doesn't have a stable grounding; it's like he's free-falling.' She sighed deeply.

'What can we do?' asked Ines.

'God, now that's a good question.'

'Hey, you, talk to us!' demanded Ines, her head thrown back, looking up at the sky.

'Do you think he'll answer?'

'No. Probably not. Would be useful though.'

'Yes, it would. Something like: *Bring the children to me!*'

'I think it goes (with a deep voice): *Let thy children come unto me,*' corrected Ines, who was surprised that after such a long time biblical citations were still hibernating inside her. 'I understand. You want to make Maxim into a little Christian and then all will be well.'

It was just a joke, but one with consequences. Sonja thought about it constantly from that day on. Without telling Ines about it, for a while.

The tide came in unbelievably quickly and, irritatingly, from all directions. They scattered and fled, leaving behind a bib, a summer hat and a corkscrew. Apart from the children, who were wearing their protective hats and outfits, everyone was sunburnt, had a burning head (Ines) or a fire red neck (Marc), saw floating spots (Chris) or felt lightheaded (Sonja). Sonja was annoyed about the picnic blanket, which had got wet despite her quick reaction. 'Until next time,' she said. 'I just want to go home. And so does Maxim.' And they were off in their own car: Sonja, Chris and Maxim. While Ines and Marc and Lilith continued to watch the tide from the safety of the car park, until the high water-level reached them.

The organ started up suddenly and with full force so that Ines jumped and Lilith woke up. Madgdalena adjusted her position, and Sonja's pale face distorted into an agonised grimace. She had chosen the music and been assured numerous times that the organist was familiar with the pieces and that he'd play them correctly and at the correct time. Yet Sonja was convinced he'd changed the programme without permission. This music was fitting for a funeral, not for a christening! It wasn't the organist's fault: he played the second movement of Mendelssohn's Organ Sonata in D as agreed. On first hearing it, Sonja had thought it sublime, celebratory and grand. *Andante con moto,* read Mendelssohn's instructions. She'd translated it as 'quiet, but with a steady movement', which at first she didn't understand, but then thought perfect for the occasion. Now she suffered with every single note, and she silently apologised to Maxim, who, compared to his mother, didn't seem to be disturbed in the slightest.

The pastor raised his arms and gestured for Sonja and Ines to stand up and step forward. It was time. Ines' heart beat fast and hard; she had the distinct impulse to flee. Just as she took the first step towards the font, Maxim in her arms, the pastor nodding at her, she suddenly felt sucked in by it all and from then everything ran like clockwork. She smiled, she squeezed Maxim's hand comfortingly, with two further exhilarated steps she arrived at her destination, the font, and discovered on closer inspection that there was nothing ridiculous about the fat angel nor did he resemble anyone she knew. His joyful face was unique and clear like the early daylight.

'Dear Mother, dear Godmother, you bring your child with you today, so that he may be baptised in the name of the Holy Trinity. Will you speak to him of God, will you draw him into the community of faith, and help him to take his place within the life and worship of Christ's Church? If so, answer, With the help of God, I will!' A little too quickly, Ines answered: 'With the help of God, I will!' She then picked up Maxim with ease, despite his fifteen kilograms and her lack of strength, and held him over the font. And in this instant, a huge shimmering bubble appeared, and inside a play was being performed: a scene from Ines' life. She saw herself sitting in the dark pantry; she saw Marc, her husband, standing on the ladder in the kitchen and Magdalena by the dining table getting up from her chair, moving the chair in front of the pantry and, sitting down again, talking through the door: 'A good evening all the way from here to in there, and how are you? What's the weather like in there? The atmosphere?' A short pause. 'I'm afraid I can't hear anything, the connection is bad right now, wait a sec, I'll just hang up and try again.' Pause. 'Ines, here speaks your bridesmaid Magdalena, perhaps you remember, almost five years ago I accompanied you to the registry office, where you married a stranger called Marc. I see it as my duty to check up again on how it's going with the marriage and if all's well with the participants. I just received extremely positive feedback from your husband Marc. He gushed about life at your side, and of course about you as an individual, so now I'm asking you. Think a bit about it and answer when I say *Go!* Go!' Ines: 'Sorry, I don't know. Everything's gone right now.' 'Gone? Fine: I, Magdalena, was invited by you, Ines, for a coffee shortly before your wedding. It was only the second time we'd met. You said you had an appointment with the goldsmith in a moment. You handed him a bundle of banknotes, he handed you a receipt and a test-ring. "Test ring?" I asked "What are you testing?" "I'm getting married," you replied. "To a man who I don't know much better than I know you. We met each other by accident two weeks ago." "I understand," I said. "That will either be really good or really terrible." You laughed. "Exactly. And I don't have a bridesmaid yet. Are you doing something on the 3rd of July?" "No," I answered. "I mean, now I do!" The third of July was a sunny, beautiful day, come on now, you know that, there were tears, champagne and bathing in the Elbe. So, my dear, now speak: Really good or really terrible?' And with these words Magdalena opened the door to the pantry and looked Ines in the eye. And Ines replied: 'Yes, I remember again. And I think it's good, thank you.' The soundtrack started to play. She got up, grabbed Magdalena and danced around in a circle with her. Marc came down from the ladder, put the cloth away and got down the wine from the shelf. 'Not for me please,' said Magdalena with a glance at the uncorked bottle. 'I've got a terrible headache and I'm going to lie down. Cheers, you two!' And Ines and Marc sat down for a long time, emptied the glasses and filled their hearts with memories, because a lot happened in five years and, it seemed to them now, they were only good things. Even when, on going up to bed, Ines looked at the ceiling and felt a stab of pain.

At this point the bubble burst and Ines felt this same stabbing again. At the same time Maxim felt so heavy in her arms she thought she might drop him at any second. She looked up and stared straight into the camera, since Magdalena had the habit of directing the lens at whatever was most important – Ines knew this because Magdalena had also filmed her wedding-day – and now the centre of attention was Maxim, whose forehead was being sprinkled with water three times by the pastor with the angel's little golden ladle, accompanied by these words: 'I baptise you in the name of the Father, the Son and the Holy Ghost,' and Ines felt caught out by the camera and smiled, even though she gritted her teeth because Maxim was growing heavier, and her strength was failing and the stabbing was getting more painful. Finally, the pastor gave the sign for her to put Maxim down. He dried his forehead and recited the baptismal words over him, which Sonja had chosen, while Ines turned to Marc and saw him whisper into Lilith's ear causing the little one to giggle terribly.

*

The day of the christening began with the nauseating discovery that the kitchen still smelt of red cabbage, and although the ceiling gleamed white, she was just waiting for tiny slimy stripes to fall onto her head, burrowing into her skin as fast and thoroughly as ticks. When such burrowing happened in her fantasies, Ines became the tick who, once stuck, could not be pulled out again. But this time Marc arrived fast enough: 'It smells here,' he confirmed in a matter-of-fact sort of way, opening the kitchen window. 'Coffee?' Ines nodded. 'But I'm going to shower first.' As she undressed, she heard Lilith squeaking and laughing in her room. She'd clearly been awake for a long time, just like Magdalena, who was playing with her and showing her the presents she'd brought with her. Ines pushed the tap completely to the left and up as far as it would go. She let the hot water stream over her head until she could no longer hear, no longer see, and, for a moment, no longer think.

*

The day of the christening began for Magdalena with the relief of realising her headache was gone. She crept into Lilith's room and watched her sleep for a while, until she couldn't bear it anymore and pinched her cheeks to see what she'd think of the presents. Lilith looked at her groggily and didn't recognise her. But after Magdalena gave her a gift, the little one said: 'Fairy! You have to stay for always, promise! Cross your heart and hope to die!' Magdalena turned up at breakfast, dressed up and ready for the event; she emphasised how she was looking forward to the christening, she so seldom had the opportunity to visit a church, and yet she loved nothing more than organ music, almost nothing, even if the opportunity was unfortunately, as she said, so seldom. She explained to Ines, when the latter worried Magdalena wasn't feeling well, that she didn't want to drink or eat anything out of concern for her lipstick and outfit.

In front of the church – where she, together with her hosts, arrived far too early – Magdalena phoned Andi, her husband. 'I'm splendid,' she said. 'My head is completely clear.' She listened for a while and repeated a little too loudly: 'I'm really fine, do you hear, I'm, I feel healthy, don't worry.' She hung up and took the camera out of the bag to prepare her contribution.

*

The day of the christening began for Sonja with the most painful thudding head she'd ever had to carry on her shoulders. Her first few steps led her to the bathroom, which was next to the kitchen-cum-dining room where her in-laws and Maxim were having breakfast. She heard her father in-law loudly pronouncing 'Strawberry jam' from the next room while she leant over the toilet bowl, lacking the strength to vomit. She also heard how Maxim tried to repeat what her grandfather said to him. But he remained stubborn. 'Straw-ber-ry ja-aa-m!' sounded again and again through the wall-tiles. Sonja remained, limp, overcome with pain, and hoping for relief, without a clear idea of what form it would take. 'Strawberry jam,' she said, joining in at some point, and that was the magic word. The contents of her stomach shot out in a quick, powerful stream into the bowl.

During this time, Chris stood on the terrace and smoked a cigarette with no hands, because the cold forced him to. The smoke went straight into his eyes, tears ran over his face.

He'd pursed his mouth in order not to lose his cigarette while smoking, and so he could warm his balled fists in his coat pockets.

'This is pathetic,' he said, when he helped Sonja up onto her feet and sloppily washed her face. She nodded. And then for hours Chris didn't say another word, but that was nothing new. They drove home in their car, where the outfits for the special day were waiting; changed, and hurried on foot to the church close by, which they reached, out of breath but on time at ten o'clock, just as the bells began to ring.

*

Lilith giggled. She couldn't calm herself, she giggled until her cheeks glowed and, despite the cold church, grew quite overheated. Ines warmed herself with the baptismal candle, which the pastor had handed to her after he'd used the Easter candle to light it. Sonja seemed to have grown paler and frantically stroked Maxim's posh side-parting while she stared blankly at the pillar where Chris had been standing. Chris was gone. He'd simply walked out. As if trying to grip hold of something which she kept sliding off, Sonja stroked Maxim's straight hair. He saw this as a sign and waved, beaming, at the circle of people with his plump little hands, both at the same time, cheerful as the angel and similarly content with himself. And the circle waved back: Granny Gitte, Grandad Hugo, Godmother Ines with the big candle, Uncle Marc with the giggling Lilith and the new Aunt Magdalena behind the camera. Magdalena hoped that it would be over soon, because a few minutes ago – and she didn't understand it herself – a strong pulsing had started in her temples after which, as a general rule, the old headache was soon to follow, and she began to find her task more difficult and wanted to sit down and get some fresh air.

Finally the organ sounded for the last time, the celebratory bracket around the font closed and the company dismissed. One followed the other out in measured steps, into the fresh air. Sonja had already prepared a little talk for Chris, which she'd deliver as soon as she met him smoking outside the church. Magdalena would have liked to find the *Fast Forward* button in order to hurry the procession and get out quicker. The organ, which she actually so liked to listen to, dampened her spirit more than the headache. Ines looked forward to picking up her unchristened daughter in her arms and throwing her into the air, which they both loved to do so much, and then to spin her around in a circle until she was dizzy or they tumbled down together. Everyone was outside now, only Chris wasn't there. Chris wasn't standing there and smoking. Chris just wasn't there anymore.

His Daughter Mascha

He blindly feels around for the key to the post-box. It's the small one with the long blade. He holds it between the thumb and forefinger of his right hand. On his left arm he carries his six-year-old daughter like he does every weekend, because she asks him to. Every Saturday, it seems to him that she's grown lighter. Still, she obscures his view and so he must put his feet down carefully and hesitantly on each step. It's much too dark in the stairwell, he thinks. When he reaches the bottom, he looks into his son's earnest eyes before he turns to the post-box on his left.

He hurriedly opens the three letters as he walks. He slits them open with the key for the post-box, his daughter on his arm, and rips out the folded pages. He does this every Saturday, even though he has time, and the children with him. As if he's waiting for urgent news he might need to respond to straightaway. As always: adverts dressed up as personal correspondence. A Whole World of Single Malt Whisky. Make the Most of Your Insurance. On the third envelope is his mother's handwriting; she's been forwarding his post once a month ever since he moved to live in a foreign country with his wife and children. Bank statements and election forms mostly. But this time: a letter from the Cemetery and Funeral Office, Zürich. The words have a strange effect on him, but he can't connect them with anything yet.

He's sitting with both kids in front of the ice cream shop. He's crying. He hopes they don't notice. The sun's shining. They've sat down outside on the terrace's pollen-dusted plastic chairs. "Look," his son gets up and points at his yellow trouser seat. "I'm in for it now." Since the beginning of the year, much to his annoyance, his son loves things to be clean and tidy, like his mother. "Watch your ice cream," he replies, "it's dripping." He's talking despite the sobs rising in his throat. "Papa, what is it?" says his daughter, surprising him. She looks worried. "What's wrong?" "Me?" He grabs the napkin and wipes her mouth.

His mother has stayed on. She still lives there, where once the whole family lived, in a plain grey house in the hilly outskirts of the city. She's been retired for a year. His young mother. She was twenty when she had him. Every time they meet he's shocked, because time hasn't stopped for her. At first glance, the young mother looks old. Then he looks into her new, old face until, after a while, he finds her familiar and young again. He imagines her before him, now that he's read the letter from the Cemetery Office. His young mother: she smiles at him sympathetically, like she did when his father died, with this strange glimmer in her eyes as if wanting to apologise, and with this vain regret around the corners of her mouth. He closes his eyes and turns away.

Mascha they would have called her; that's what they'd decided, his then-girlfriend and him. Still underage, both of them, just left school and looking forward to everything that life could offer. Was that really twenty-five years ago? Mascha would have been older now than her mother was, back then. His daughter, would she have been twenty-five today? He shakes his head. "What's wrong," asks his daughter again, the six year old. "Karla," he answers, "I love you."

He watches his son peer at a bike shop on the other side of the road. From behind, his shoulder blades seem so fragile. On the back of his light-coloured trousers, the formerly yellow pollen-dust begins to show as a frayed browned stain. He can make out racing bikes with paper-thin wheels through the window. Is his son interested in cycling? What does 'would' mean, he suddenly thinks, she *was* called Mascha. The name 'Mascha Wehrli' is on her gravestone. Wehrli was her mother, who he hasn't heard from for – how long was it again? At least ten years – no, wait – longer, it had to be much longer ago. Mascha brought them together; Mascha pulled them apart, once and for all.

1985! He remembers that New Year's Eve; he sees Mascha's mother coming towards him from the bargain-shop with a bottle of wine like a trophy, smiling triumphantly in her shapeless black persian coat. The coat gapes open over her stomach. The ball, he thinks, is coming towards me. The ball: Mascha.

He remembers how he used to think the persian coat smelt like a grave, like moist, clammy decay. Karla sits on his lap and scrapes the ice cream bowl with her little spoon. She seems distant, and sighs for no reason.

The period of burial has expired, writes the Cemetery Authority. Eternal peace is over. He grimaces as if the thought makes him sick. They have been generous, write the Cemetery Authority, as is well-known, the legal period of burial constitutes twenty years and has therefore been exceeded by five years. *As is well-known*; he winces.

The corpse will remain untouched in the earth. The gravestone can be collected on presenting the enclosed document. *Untouched,* he wants to curl his lip, but sees his son's earnest gaze on him. "Do you like them?" he asks, nodding to the racing bikes on the other side of the street, and feels foolish.

His mother forwarded the letter without opening it. But she would have seen the stamp – City of Zürich – Department of Population Affairs, Cemetery and Funeral Office on the envelope. And now? Would Mascha's mother receive the same letter? Impossible. He was the one responsible for the gravesite. He counts the twenty-five years and he's shocked by it: a grave administered by means of standing order, even if he hasn't once in all these years visited the cemetery. Mascha, his daughter. Mascha. She could be the mother of his daughter, Karla. She could be his wife. He plays through the possibilities in his mind and uses the image of Mascha's mother. Or his lover. No. Stop. Over. She could be his daughter. Mascha: still-born on the 9th May 1985. It's become quiet. He sees his son sitting at the table again, and he nudges Karla on his lap: 'Can you manage another ice cream?' He can suddenly see laughter like a light come over his son's face, and Karla starts kicking her legs. I've found the switch, he thinks.

White and Black

Ninety-five per cent of all acoustic stimulus is not relayed to one's consciousness. We are only made aware of sounds which are classified as important. For example, in a crowd of talking people, a listener's attention will be immediately caught by someone saying their name, and he will automatically turn to face the speaker.

I wish that someone would say my name, so that my attention might be caught and I'd turn to face the speaker *automatically*. The neck of the beer bottle has grown warm in my fist, with my free hand I stroke my neck, and I feel like screaming, quick and piercing.

'Everything in the universe is just – a standing wave.' I recognise this voice. This masculine alto. Nine words have intruded into my consciousness, even though my name wasn't mentioned. I have deemed an acoustic stimulus to be important. This high masculine voice.

'The standing wave points to equilibrium. Resonance.'

My eyes search for owner of the voice; he looks at me. The man who's crossed my path, again and again, for years. The man who has a face, but no name. Only a nickname: Snow White. A pale face, white as snow; hair and eyes black as ebony, and the voice of a woman. Snow White. He's turned

145

away from the person opposite him and is looking at me. He's looking at me through thick glasses with tiny black eyes as he talks on, clear and high. 'Without resonance you can end up homesick, for instance. You long for the place where you and the ground move together, where the surface of your body and that of the soil are the same. You want to be in equilibrium with the world.' He smiles at me, his tiny round eyes gleam black behind his glasses. 'If you've traveled through the whole world without having found equilibrium, then that's tough luck. If you're still homesick, then nothing in this world can help you. Then you're homesick for – no idea, the underworld?' He laughs angelically, leaves his partner standing at the bar, and comes over to me with a beer bottle raised in his hand.

'Hey,' he says. 'Hey,' I say.

He hits the top of my beer bottle vertically with the bottom of his. 'Cheers.' The beer in my bottle fizzes over. 'Standing wave,' says the angelic voice. He laughs, taking the bottle from me, licks the foam and says, 'Come on, we're going.' And we go.

*

There's a man lying in my bath, black and white. The whiteness of his skin has a blue tinge like diluted milk. The blackness of his head, chest and pubic area has no clear outline. I've taken off my glasses, which gives things their clarity, contour and edges. The rampant blackness threatens to eat up the milk-whiteness: three black bushes at the head, chest and pubic area, which have all settled down with this white host and are spreading out at his expense.

He pretends to be a dead man, showing the whites of his

eyes, mouth open, a red hole. Snow White; dead man. The hole narrows. 'I'm freezing,' he says. 'Get in.'

Our clothes lie on the tiles. We undressed in time with each other. At the end he took off his glasses and said, 'seven diopters.' 'Five,' I said and put my glasses next to his in the sink. We laughed. A Duet. Soprano and Alto.

'You're beautiful,' he said.

'You can't see anything.'

'True.' We laughed.

'Your voice...'

'Alto,' he replied. He gave himself two short blows with both palms on his chest and loins, 'but I'm a man and that's all there is to it.' As I got into the bath, he sang somewhere between G and treble C, 'Yes, I'm a man, that's all there is, all there is.' Then he panted, 'co-co-co-cold,' and jumped from one foot to the other, slipped and fell.

I look at him. He does the dead man. Only his white penis moves slightly in the water. 'Look out, he's swimming away,' I say. He grabs his dick with his white hand and holds it tight. 'I'm freezing! Just get in.'

I'm not sure when we met each other for the first time. If it's true that we're not aware of ninety-five per cent of acoustic stimulus, how much or how little would it be for optical stimulus? For years, our meetings were nothing other than sightings. I saw him, nothing more. At some point I became aware of seeing him. Then I realised that I wasn't seeing him for the first time. *It's him. Him again.*

The earliest sighting I remember was five years ago.

I sat in silence with David in a café. Suddenly he was standing there, casually leaning against the doorframe, his feet crossed at the ankles, looking at us with his tiny eyes through his thick glasses. Years passed. I saw him at the bus stop, in the park, in the tram, on a station platform, at a supermarket checkout, in the cinema foyer, in cafés. And he – casually leaning against door frames, bus stops, trees and fences, his feet crossed at the ankles – watched us. With tiny glimmering black eyes. He watched us, because I was never alone when I saw him. When his swan-like eyes looked at me, us. My father and I. David and I. Us.

It took a long time before I heard his voice, this far too high masculine voice. I sat in the tram with my father. He stood in front, by the door, casually leaning against the hand-rail, and said to a man who bumped into him as he got off: 'Good luck and may your life be blessed.'

I listened, nudged my father and laughed. The swan-eyes glanced at us.

As the years went by, I heard his voice again and again, but it never spoke to me, or to us. It spoke with traffic wardens, begging junkies, disorientated grandmas, cheeky kids, badly behaved dogs and their owners.

On the other hand, he was always looking at me: me and David, me and father. They're dead, David and my father.

When my father refused to shake hands with his fellow human beings, he'd refer to Nikolas Tesla. Apparently, he always maintained a metre distance from other people, because the unfamiliar magnetic fields disturbed him. That my father would, despite this, sometimes touch or embrace me, I took as a sign of love. He'd speak of his life as a wasted one. 'Do it better, child,' he often said with relish, when we raised our brandy glasses and looked into each other's eyes. Instead of earning money, he should have taken care of the legacy of Nikolas Tesla's work, he said. He didn't doubt that he was

Tesla's legitimate, equal, yes, genius successor. Even though, to my knowledge my father knew nothing of the natural sciences. But at least he had subscribed to a Nature and Science Magazine. I always used to see the current issue lying on the kitchen table in his tiny flat when I visited him and we drank cognac together. He would have led a meaningful life in Tesla's footsteps, he said. If my father had been granted another life, he would have immediately put into action Tesla's *Worldwide Energy and Communication System*, which, he said, should solve all the problems of energy supply. My father died suddenly a year ago.

It was a year after David's death. He had lost his life in a motorbike accident. Until then we shared the same table, bed, loves, fears. When I'd come home in the evening, he'd share the fruits of his thinking with me. He'd ruminate about the future. At the start, when we were just getting to know each other, he'd explained how God had left him the moment his voice had broken. Free from faith, he'd immediately begun to think. He pursued two types of questions about the future for as long as I knew him. The first: 'What will I experience in my life?' And the second: 'What if?' He began with dinner. I ate, he talked. 'What would happen if food were cheap, free from harmful substances, delicious, and made solely in laboratories? World hunger would be solved. And we'd bid farewell to Mother Earth. Both would bring about unbelievable changes, good and bad. That will be it, the oft-proclaimed downfall of the West!' He cried out in excitement.

Of course, my favourite questions were about his own future. When, at dinner, he asked me in all seriousness: 'I wonder if I'll ever commit murder?' we'd be sure to have a long, lively and fun evening together.

I squint at Snow White through wet eyelashes. With every blink I see him, see myself, see my dead loved-ones.

Him loitering in the doorway;

David next to me in the cinema;

Me at the bus stop;

My father on the station platform, hugging me goodbye;

Me on the platform, I'm being hugged and I smell the wet material of my father's trench-coat;

Him loitering at a supermarket check-out;

David in the supermarket, searching in vain for some money;

Me in the supermarket, handing David the money he hands over to the woman at the till;

Me in the supermarket; I see him, Snow White, leaning casually against the check-out, and me looking on, us, David and me.

It's narrow in the bath. I squint at him. We're squatting opposite each other, shivering, our torsos and knees protruding out of the water. 'Do you remember,' I shake my head to clear the water from my eyelashes to see more clearly, 'do you remember watching me and my father saying goodbye on the platform?'

'No,' he says, and pulls his leg out of the water; squeaking, I slide in deeper.

'No?'

'No.'

He stretches his foot towards me. The foot is longer than my face. It's an angel's foot. The sole is soft and tender like a new-born's. This virginal sole hasn't yet touched the ground or carried the weight of a body. It comes nearer and nearer to my eyes and places itself on my face, a wonderfully soft cloth, and presses me slowly and relentlessly under the water, until the back of my head hits the bottom of the bathtub. A hard metallic Ping! thuds inside my skull. I try and pull myself up, the sole hits me again and again – ping, ping, ping. 'You're killing me!' I gurgle under the water, spluttering. 'Sure,' I hear him say, bright and easy.

Snow White was David's suggestion. While the swearing David was trying to start his motorbike, I spotted him leaning nonchalantly against a one-way sign a few metres away, watching us: David cursing, and me, standing and waiting uselessly at David's side, doing nothing. Snow White watched us through breath-misted glasses. When David finally and triumphantly turned around to face me, saying, 'Let's go, get on!', he had disappeared. 'Do you know that man?' I asked David, 'The man who was watching us and who disappeared just now?'

'I didn't see him, love, I was busy,' said David. 'Now come on, get on!'

'He had black hair, black eyes and snow-white skin and a woman's voice.'

'Then it was probably Snow White,' said David, revving the engine. 'Come on, get your butt over here!'

I squint at him through wet eyelashes. 'Snow White.' He makes smacking noises in the water through little, tender movements of the palms of his hands.

'You,' he says. I shake my head. 'No, you.'

'Youuuuu,' he sings from his chest. His mouth wide open, a red hole. His finger beckons me to sing along, get in tune. 'You,' I sing. I sing the same tone. The range of both our voices put together averages around ten notes. He's chosen the deepest tone for both of us, because the deeper notes suit the bathroom better. Apparently that's why men like to sing in the bath so much. But the reasons why men love to sing so joyfully in the bathroom seems to be a complex field, which cannot be adequately explained by their deeper tone of voice. As Snow White is now proving.

'Youuuuuuuuuuuu,' we sing, while his finger conducts.

'That's it,' he says. 'The standing wave.'

The sound echoes against the tiled walls: my You, his You, the You of the walls which pile on top of each other to create a rising, giant You.

He's laughing with his cave-like mouth, nodding enthusiastically, 'Youuuuuu.' The finger stops moving. The You echoes and fades away. The cave-like mouth comes towards me. A red tongue-tip touches my bottom lip. 'You,' he says. 'If we could keep on singing and hold the note without losing it, we could make the bathroom collapse.' We laugh as if in a duet. 'Imagine the ruins. Our crushed bodies. Youuuuuuu,' he cries, and there it is, the standing wave, there it is again. I peer upwards.

The tone fades away, the ceiling remains. We've survived our sing-song. We crouch opposite each other, his blue-tinged shimmering knee against mine, pairing up knee to knee. I look in the direction where I assume his eyes are. Two short-sighted people in a bath; we're looking straight at each other, but still can't see anything. We look at each other in silence.

'Now listen to me for a moment,' he says, as if I've been interrupting him the whole time. 'The bathroom could only collapse in an ideal world.'

He pauses.

'Light knows no loss. Noise, on the other hand, sound, song, language, the spoken word – nothing but loss, loss, loss.'

Silence.

'And yet: It's better to make this bathroom collapse than our hearts. If something should come up which meets your heart's own frequency – something which makes your heart start to swing and dance – then it would be nothing more but a misunderstanding.'

Silence.

His round shining swan's eyes are blurred stains. We look, yet don't see each other. He can see less of me than I him.

'I'm freezing,' he pushes the temperature gauge to the left with his angel's foot and tilts it upwards. I try and avoid the jet of hot water, which forces me to move in between his legs towards the wallowing white dick. 'He who's blind, must feel,' he laughs, grabs the back of my neck and pulls me towards him.

'Do you remember?' I ask. 'My companion?'

'I do remember then.'

'When?'

'Then.'

'Look at me.'

'Why?' He asks.

We laugh, clear and dark, and the bath overflows.

Snow White lies in my bed, white and black, eyes closed, on his back. The arms are stretched to the side, two wings; an angel who's standing in mid-air. He hums quietly and lightly through his closed mouth. I kneel next to him and look at him: he who can't remember. Look at him, caress with my eyes his tender white skin and think of all the things his eyes have seen. Think of those he can't remember. He hums, I nuzzle him with my eyes, project onto his white skin the images of my loved-ones and say, in my mind. *You are a witness, Snow*

White. And you don't remember my father, who I resemble so closely? Nor David, my – David in black leather, who I – you saw us, watched us. Observed us. You can't do that – you can't just have forgotten them!

He lies there and hums. My dead ones look at me as if stuck to a postcard: with best wishes from the underworld. Helpless and stupid, smiling at the camera and at me, blushing red in a trench-coat, in black leathers. Snow White has his eyes closed, humming.

We ran across the hallway towards the bed, hand in hand, naked and wet. I turned around and looked back at our footprints on the wood. 'Onwards!' he said and ran into the door frame. 'Left, this way!' I pulled him to my side and into bed.

'I'm freezing,' he says, with his eyes closed. I lie on top of him. He hums on, an octave deeper. His skin is smooth and cool like paper. I lay my cheek on his breast-bone, hear the humming grow fuller and deeper, and look past his shoulder at the vacant white wall. Our glasses are still in the sink. 'He who can't see, must smell and taste,' he says. I sniff his shoulder. 'Yes,' he says, 'go on.' I can't smell anything. A hint of soap, then nothing. I sniff at his forehead, nose, ears, lips, neck, and smell nothing. My nose wanders over his black-haired chest and navel to his dick, which, well embedded, shines from its dark nest. I smell nothing. He smells of nothing. No hint of anything, apart from a whiff of soap, which I subtract from my smell-impression. 'Go on, carry on,' he says. I sniff at his balls and thighs, the white knees, the black hair on his calves, his shins, ankles, angel's feet. Nothing. I'm smelling a man who does not smell. I lick his body with my tongue, from bottom to top, crisscrossing. Nothing. I taste nothing. This un-smell, this un-taste disgusts me.

'I'm freezing.' With one move, I climb on top of him and straddle him, sitting on his groin. He opens his mouth and quietly groans, 'Ouch.' He opens his eyes, the black of his irises flash with anger. He throws me off with one jerk off his loins and hurls himself at me.

I close my eyes and mouth. I see David in front of me, a figure in black leather with a motorbike helmet. He takes off the helmet and smiles, *hey,* he says, *let's go!* Snow White lies on top of me, I smile at David. We move up and down. An inkling of a smell arrives at my nose. With the scent comes a memory. Images of the beloved dead – of me, him – they're overlapping. I embrace my father and I feel David's dick in me and I hear his voice: *It's a shame actually, if I ever get to know about it, it'll be too late.* And the postcards come to life, take off their coats, pass me by, kiss me, look at me, blush, smile, speak. My father says: *Do it better, child, do it better.*

Let's go, says David and gets on the motorbike. *Goooo!*

I open my eyes. Snow White is staring at me. 'Don't you remember?' I ask him. He turns his head away. I grab his chin. He resists. I grasp it hard and turn his head. 'No,' he says. My hand slips down easily to his throat. He says my name. I press down hard and he doesn't resist.

Dinner with Dürrenmatt

My mother wasn't there the time my godfather and his wife, the woman from Appenzell, invited me out for dinner. My mother wasn't there, yet she's the one who reminds me of it. She's the one who tells me what I – following that dinner in the *Kronenhalle* a good ten years back – once told her, and which then, I think, I immediately forgot. How did we ever come to talk about it? My godfather, his wife from Appenzell, the *Kronenhalle*? By chance, of course. The existence of every story owes more to chance than to its narrator.

My story was already as good as finished: a story about a place of longing called the *Kronenhalle,* named after the old Zürich restaurant with its famous clientele. A place I'd never been to, but which was always available to me in the treasure chest or larder of my imagination, appearing like a stage-set whenever I felt subdued. If there was a meeting planned with the beloved dead, for instance. A cultivated dinner with Dürrenmatt, for instance. Whom I'd turn into a godfather, if I didn't have one already. Uncle Fritz. I'd do it without asking, of course. That's the prerogative of the living. The dead are taken over – that's the way it is, that's the way it ought to be.

My story was as good as finished, but then came Easter.

In the morning, I leave a message for my mother on the Zürich answer machine. She calls Hamburg back in the afternoon. One doesn't know where one stands, she says, "alternating bright blue and threatening dark skies. And with you?"

"Cool and windy of course, and grey," I say. "Reliably grey."

She laughs. "Talking about the weather."

"In Dürrenmatt, the weather conditions and the general state of the world are connected."

"Reality is complicated," she replies.

"It occurs to me now, because I'm just in the middle of writing a story…"

"About the weather?"

"About the *Kronenhalle*."

Silence.

"The restaurant," I add.

"Aha." She draws out the final 'a', long and high.

An hour later we say goodbye and hang up. For an hour, my mother told me what I'd forgotten: that there'd been a dinner, an invitation from my godfather and his wife, the woman from Appenzell, who was once his secretary, to eat together in the *Kronenhalle*, no less, a real treat. There was no better occasion for it: my father's death, a kind of funereal feast, since we hadn't met at the actual funeral itself. Yes, it's unfortunate, and his death is a great loss. In some ways, he was the link between us, the godfather and his god-daughter, but now he's dead and gone forever. You had to be there at the graveside to understand what can't be understood (the woman from Appenzell nods in agreement): that he, the link, is no longer in existence (the woman from Appenzell shakes her head in disbelief). And us – he, the Uncle and I, the child – now just two loose ends, right? Regret in her voice, a frown on her nodding head and a heavy sigh. Another glass of wine – yes? A subtle hand gesture; a woman from Appenzell, who understands it straightaway; a waiter, who is called.

My mother tells me all this with such ease it takes my breath away. After ten years, she tells me again what I told her, just like that, on the phone from over eight hundred and sixty-six kilometres away: she parades it before my eyes, resurrects and brings to life what I'd lost: my own story, the story of the end of Godparenthood. The longer she talks, the more I nod, think and feel and know and I say: "Yes, yes, that's what it was like." As if the story had matured in her cellar and now, at exactly the right time, it's brought upstairs, opened and served.

I can suddenly remember the wine, taste its bitterness, see the woman from Appenzell's violet lips and I automatically run my tongue over my own; I hear her metallic voice saying: "If you're not going to eat anything, we shouldn't have come to the *Kronenhalle*,"; see my godfather's warning look, which silences her, and my answer: "I just don't eat meat. I never have." I see them both nod, even though it's obvious neither of them understand and that they find it completely ridiculous. "Then you don't have much joy in life," says the woman from Appenzell, jumping in her seat, because my Uncle may have kicked her a little too hard under the table. I look at her and answer: "No." And there's a pause which is awkward for all three of us and so creates a kind of small togetherness.

My mother tells me this forgotten story in such a way that

it makes me laugh. She waits until the line is quiet again before saying: "The end was abrupt. Through the use of a gesture you hardly recognised, he sent the woman from Appenzell to pay, followed her with his eyes and supervised her actions, which unfortunately took place behind your back, while he tried to distract you with dull questions about your future plans. When the woman from Appenzell returned to the table, he leapt up, helped her into her coat and said: 'Of coure, we can give you a lift home.'" Yes, that's how it happened, and no, I never heard from my godfather and his wife from Appenzell again. And they never heard from me either.

But I have an entirely different problem now. Before the conversation with my mother on the phone, I was sure I'd never been to the *Kronenhalle*. And now, after the call, I've got this story hanging like a millstone round my neck! A story which intrudes on my already completed story about the place of longing called the *Kronenhalle*; a place which, in reality I'd never been to, a place where I liked to meet dead writers and poets for dinner. Dürrenmatt, for instance.

Now there are two *Kronenhalle* in my life: one real and one fictional. As usual, reality is not as beautiful, and fiction is my elixir for survival. Here, the reality, where I lost my godfather; there, the fictional, where I was almost on first name terms with Dürrenmatt (from where the step to calling him 'Friedrich' and then 'Uncle Fritz' would have been tiny).

By the way, Dürrenmatt – I can reveal this much about the first story – acts like a regular, and seems to be one. He talks a little too loudly, especially when he calls the waiting staff by name; he definitely laughs too loudly, particularly when he tells a joke; he attacks his food with a shameless appetite, and he critiques what he's still chewing; he grunts; he sticks his right forefinger into the back of his mouth, while his left beckons people over; he gawps shamelessly at the woman at the next table; he asks me why I'm looking at him funny, and laughs (definitely too loudly); he whispers: "Don't turn round now," and observes what I can't see, because I obey him; he whistles vulgarly and says a word used to describe the reproductive organs of a male farm animal, but which he applies to a person; he turns to me and asks softly, what we'd been talking about.

Meanwhile the *Voiture* has been rolling by again and again on its invisible tracks, which he – with a raised hand and a long-drawn out "Wait" as if he were a tram-conductor (even without cap and signalling baton) – has stopped several times, so that the trolley-lady may open the silver-plated cloches and present him with steaming meats, of which he selects morsels, polishing them off before he returns, or is able to return, to speaking of relevant subjects pertaining to matters of the real world.

When I ask myself now how it began, how and when our *Kronenhalle* meetings took their course, I have a simple answer: it began with a reading from *The Promise*. As is well-known, *The Promise* consists of a car journey from Chur to Zürich, and includes a lengthy meal at the *Kronenhalle* where both "heroes" tell each other a story. (The person to whom the story is being told writes it down afterwards and publishes it under the name Friedrich Dürrenmatt and under the title, *The Promise*). The story itself takes place in a little town called Mägendorf. Mägendorf near Zürich. Pure fiction, as our German teacher proved by means of a political map of the canton of Zürich during the reading. "A town with this name does not exist," she breathed with her coffee breath. But for me, Mägendorf was just as real as the *Kronenhalle*, which, back then I guessed was probably *pure fiction* from Dürrenmatt as well (and a good thing too, as far as I was concerned). The *Kronenhalle* was just as real as the teacher's coffee breath. There was no point closing your eyes to it: both would just grow more intense, the teacher's breath and the images of the restaurant's interior. And I wished I was there – not with the teacher's breath, no! Not at Mägendorf either – watch out! Girls were murdered in Mägendorf as we all know. I wished I was at the *Kronenhalle*, sitting at a table laid for dinner. Because that's where stories were told: stories which, as Dürrenmatt writes at the end of *The Promise:* "You can do with what you like."

PARTHIAN

the Carriage
Stone.
Sigbjørn
Hølmebakk

Translated from the Norwegian
by Frances D. Vardamm

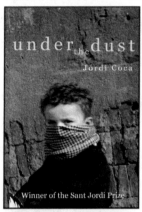

under the dust

Jordi Coca

Winner of the Sant Jordi Prize

PAPER
SPURS
OLGA MERINO

STRANGE
LANGUAGE

RAREBIT

NEW
WELSH
FICTION

EDITED BY SUSIE WILD

THE HOUSE
OF THE
DEAF MAN
Peter
KRIŠTÚFEK

TRANSLATION